Alan Bennett started his writing and performing life in reviews for the Cambridge Footlights. *Forty Years On*, his first stage play, was first produced in 1968 and since then he has become one of Britain's most popular theatre and television writers. His plays include *Forty Years On*, *Single Spies* and *The Old Country*. He has also written two widely acclaimed screenplays, *A Private Function* and *Prick Up Your Ears*, and more recently, for television, a series of six monologues, *Talking Heads*. He also presented Channel 4's series *Poetry in Motion*.

by the same author

plays
FORTY YEARS ON with GETTING ON,
HABEAS CORPUS and ENJOY
THE OLD COUNTRY
OFFICE SUITE
TWO KAFKA PLAYS
SINGLE SPIES
THE MADNESS OF GEORGE III

television plays
THE WRITER IN DISGUISE
OBJECTS OF AFFECTION (BBC)
TALKING HEADS (BBC)

screenplays
A PRIVATE FUNCTION
PRICK UP YOUR EARS

autobiography
THE LADY IN THE VAN (LRB)

THE WIND IN
THE WILLOWS
by KENNETH GRAHAME

adapted by
Alan Bennett

faber and faber
LONDON · BOSTON

First published in 1991
by Faber and Faber Limited
3 Queen Square London WC1N 3AU

Photoset by Parker Typesetting Service Leicester
Printed in England by Clays Ltd St Ives plc

Adaptation of *The Wind in the Willows* © Forelake Limited, 1991
Based on the original novel by Kenneth Grahame
Introduction © Alan Bennett, 1991
Lyrics to 'Camp Fire Song' and 'Happy to Float' © Jeremy Sams, 1991

A CIP record for this book is available from the British Library

ISBN 0-571-16458-7

4 6 8 10 9 7 5 3

CONTENTS

The Wind in the Willows was first performed at the Royal National Theatre, London, on 12 December 1990. The cast included:

The River Bank

MOLE	David Bamber
RAT	Richard Briers
TOAD	Griff Rhys Jones
BADGER	Michael Bryant
OTTER	John Matshikiza
ALBERT	Terence Rigby
RABBITS	Chris Larner, Charlotte Medcalf, David Joyce, Tricia Morrish, Nicholas Monu, Derek Smee
HEDGEHOGS	Nick Holder, Mike Murray, Judith Coke, Mona Hammond
SQUIRRELS	Sue Devaney, Raymond Platt, Guy Moore
FIELDMICE, SMALL RABBITS, SMALL SQUIRRELS, BILLY, TOMMY and PORTLY	Finchley Children's Music Group.

The Wild Wood

CHIEF WEASEL	Tim McMullan
WEASEL NORMAN	Adrian Scarborough
GERALD FERRET	David Joyce
SERGEANT FRED FERRET	Chris Larner
FOX	Derek Smee
THE VOICE OF PAN	Duncan Bell

The Wide World

PARKINSON	Guy Moore
RUPERT	Raymond Platt
MONICA	Judith Coke
MAGISTRATE	John Nettleton
CLERK OF THE COURT	Mike Murray
POLICEMAN	Nicholas Monu
GAOLER'S DAUGHTER	Sue Devaney
WASHERWOMAN	Mona Hammond
GUARD	Adrian Scarborough
TRAIN DRIVER	Nick Holder
TICKET CLERK	Derek Smee
BARGEWOMAN	Carol Macready
GYPSY	James Goode

Musicians   Keith Thompson, Sarah Clarke, Anna Hemery, David Joyce, Chris Larner, Charlotte Medcalf, Tricia Morrish, Michael S. Murray, Jane Sebba

Director	Nicholas Hytner
Designer	Mark Thompson
Lighting	Paul Pyant
Music and Additional Lyrics	Jeremy Sams
Music Director	Keith Thompson
Fights and Stunts	Johnny Hutch
Director of Movement	Jane Gibson
Company Voice Work	Patsy Rodenburg

INTRODUCTION

Some time in 1987 Richard Eyre, newly appointed Director of the National Theatre, asked me if I'd think about writing a play that would combine *The Wind in the Willows* with some account of the life of its author Kenneth Grahame. I had one or two similar approaches around that time, including a proposal for a film in which Bob Hoskins was to play Rat and Michael Caine Toad. Kenneth Grahame died in 1932, so this flurry of interest could be put down to money and managements waking up to the fact that, fifty years on, here was a best-seller that was now out of copyright.

Cut to December 1990, a week before the opening of the play I eventually wrote. Passing the British Museum, I ran into Bodley's Librarian, David Vaisey, who was taking a gloomy breather from some unending committee on the impending transfer to the new British Library. As I told him about rehearsing *The Wind in the Willows*, he became gloomier still. What I had not known was that Kenneth Grahame's long love affair with Oxford had led him to bequeath the copyright in the book to the university, and a good little earner it had proved to be. Now the National Theatre's gain was about to be the Bodleian Library's loss.

I don't recall reading *The Wind in the Willows* as a child, or indeed any of the classics of children's literature. This was partly the library's fault. In those days Armley Junior Library at the bottom of Wesley Road in Leeds bound all their volumes in heavy maroon or black, so that *The Adventures of Milly Molly Mandy* were every bit as forbidding as *The Anatomy of Melancholy*. Doubtless *The Wind in the Willows* was there somewhere, along with *Winnie the Pooh* and *Alice* and all the other books every well-brought-up *Children's Hour*-listening child was supposed to read. Actually, I think I do remember looking at *Alice* and being put off by the Tenniel illustrations. 'Too old fashioned,' I thought, 'looks like a classic,' and back it went on the shelf.

It was only in the sixties, when I was rather haphazardly reading round the Edwardians with some vague idea of writing a history play, (which eventually turned into *Forty Years On*), that I read Kenneth Grahame's *The Golden Age* and *Dream Days*. I left *The Wind in the Willows* until last because I thought I had read it already – this being virtually the definition of a classic: a book everyone is assumed to have read and often thinks they have done so.

One consideration that had kept me away from the book for so long, gave it a protective coating every bit as off-putting as those black and maroon bindings of my childhood, was that it had *fans*. Fans are a feature of a certain kind of book. It's often a children's book – *Winnie the Pooh*, *Alice* and *The Hobbit* are examples – or it is a grown-up children's book such as those of Wodehouse, E. F. Benson and Conan Doyle. But Jane Austen and Anthony Trollope are nothing if not adult and they have fans too – and fan clubs – so children are not the essence of it.

What is common to all these authors, though, is the capacity to create self-contained worlds; their books constitute systems of literary self-sufficiency in ways that other novels, often more profound, do not. It is a kind of cosiness. Dickens is not cosy; he is always taking his reader back into the real world in a way that Trollope, who is cosy, does not. So it is Trollope who has the fans. In our own day the same distinction could be drawn between the novels of Evelyn Waugh and those of Anthony Powell – Powell with fans, Waugh not. And though exceptions occur to me even as I write – the Brontës? (Fans of the lives more than of the books.) Hardy? (Fans of the scenery) – I have always found fans a great deterrent: 'It's just your kind of thing.' 'Really? And how would you know?'

Back in 1988, I set to work trying to interweave Grahame's real and fictional worlds, but I soon ran into difficulties. Grahame's life had not been a happy one. Born in 1859, he never had (as he put it) 'a proper equipment of parents', and was effectively orphaned at the age of five when his mother died of scarlet fever and his drunkard father packed him off to Cookham in Berkshire to live with his grandparents; he never saw his father again. He was sent to St Edward's School in Oxford, where he did moderately well, and was looking forward to going up to university there when the family – or the 'grown-ups', as he thought of them all his life – decided he should go into the City as a clerk ('a pale-faced quilldriver') in the Bank of England.

Disappointed though he was (and it was a disappointment that did not fade), Grahame did well at the Bank, and eventually became Secretary at the early age of thirty-nine. Still, for all his conventional appearance (and despite the 'Kitchener Needs You' moustache), he was hardly a conscientious clerk, and even in those relaxed days, soon acquired a reputation for sloping off early. When he was at his desk, he was often not doing the Bank's work but writing articles for the *National Observer* and *The Yellow Book*. Pretty conventional for the most part, his pieces deplored the creeping tide of suburbia and extolled the charms of the countryside, sentiments that have been familiar and fashionable ever since, although nowadays Grahame's style is somewhat hard to take.

Grahame himself comes over as a sympathetic character who, even when he begins to acquire a literary reputation, still has about him the air of a humble clerk, tied to his desk and longing to escape – like those little men on the loose that crop up in Wells or, later, in Priestley and Orwell. Of course, it is easier if you are an animal: his draper's shop has to burn down and his death be assumed before Mr Polly can escape; with Mole, it is just a matter of flinging aside his duster and brush, saying, 'Hang spring-cleaning!' and then up he comes into the sunlight and finds himself in 'the warm grass of a great meadow' . . . and a new life.

A new life of a different sort began for Grahame in 1899, when he was forty. Hitherto very much the bachelor, he suddenly – and to the surprise and consternation of his friends – became engaged to Elspeth Thompson, whom in due course he rather resignedly married. A Scot like himself, she was fey as well as formidable – insisting, for instance, on wearing a daisy chain to their wedding – but though their courtship had been conducted largely in baby talk, there does not seem to have been much talk about babies afterwards. Sex did not come up to the expectations of either of them, but before it was discontinued, they had one quick child, Alastair, who was born premature and half blind.

He was a precocious boy, though – Elspeth, in particular, insisting on his charm and ability – with the result that he was much spoiled and given to tantrums, during which he would beat his head on the ground in fits of grief and rage. When his father started to write letters to him telling the stories that, in 1908, became *The Wind in the Willows*, Mr Toad's tantrums were intended to ring a bell.

The book was far from being an immediate success ('As a contribution to natural history,' wrote *The Times* critic, 'the book is negligible'), but at least this saved Alastair Grahame from the fate of A. A. Milne's son Christopher Robin, dogged always by his fictional counterpart. Still there was not much else that went right for Alastair. Since his father had longed to go to Oxford, Alastair was sent there, but as the child of eccentric parents and lacking any social skills, he was as unhappy as he had been at Eton and, in 1920, was found dead on the railway line that runs by Port Meadow in Oxford.

The ironies are dreadful: the river bank, setting of the father's idyll, scene of the son's death; the train, Mr Toad's deliverer, the instrument of the real-life Mr Toad's destruction. Though these tragic events were made the substance of an excellent radio play – *The Killing of Toad* by David Gooderson – I found it impossible to imagine them incorporated in *The Wind in the Willows* without casting a dark shadow over that earthly paradise – and so the project lapsed.

In March 1990, at the suggestion of Nicholas Hytner, the National revived the idea of an adaptation of Grahame's book, only this time in the form of a Christmas show that would be virtually all sunlight and would display to advantage all the technical capabilities of the Olivier stage.

My theatrical imagination is pretty limited. It is all I can do to get characters on to the stage. Once they are there, I can never think of a compelling reason for them to leave – 'I think I'll go now' being the nearest I get to dramatic urgency. So I was too set in my ways to be instantly liberated by the technological opportunities of the commission.

'But there's a caravan in it,' I remember complaining, 'what do we do about that?'

'I'm sure it's possible,' comforted Nicholas Hytner, who is

accustomed to launching 747s from the stage. 'Just write it in.'

'But it's drawn by a *horse*,' I persisted. 'We can't have a real horse and we can't have a pantomime horse or else we'll have to have a pantomime Rat and Mole and Badger.'

'Who is this idiot?' would have been a permissible response, but Nicholas Hytner patiently explained that there were several actors who looked like carthorses and who would take the part very well. It was all so simple, just as long as one used the imagination.

I set this down more or less as it happened, in case there should be any budding playwrights more tentative than I am. It's unlikely. I've been at it now for twenty-five years and if I still can't stretch my mind to envisage a man playing a horse, what have I learned?

After that, though, it all came much easier. When the motor car appeared, I just wrote '*A motor car comes on*', and likewise with the barge. The only thing the designer Mark Thompson was dubious about – on grounds of expense – was the railway train, but by that time I had got the bit between my teeth and wrote the scene in which Toad is rescued by the train with the note: 'I think you can suggest a train with clouds of steam, hooters, etc.' Etcetera.

These props, and particularly the car and the train, were splendidly done and handsomely finished. As Griff Rhys Jones (who played Toad) remarked, most stage props look worse the closer you get to them, whereas these stood up to the actors' closest scrutiny, being beautifully detailed in places (such as the dashboard of the car) that the audience can scarcely hope to see.

To understand the technical side of the production, one needs to know that the stage of the Olivier comprises an inner circle and an outer circle. The meadow on which much of the action takes place was built on the inner circle; round and slightly crumpled in appearance, it was generally referred to by the crew as 'The Poppadum'. Around this, the outer circle – a rim about six and a half feet wide – did duty as river or road. Both inner and outer circles can revolve in either direction, and the inner circle can rise or fall, either one half at a time or in one piece, when it resembles a huge hollow drum. Thus when the scene changed to Rat's house, the inner circle revolved and the drum rose at the same time, to reveal the interior of the house beneath the meadow, the combination of the stage rising and revolving making the scene appear to spiral up into view. A similar transformation took place when Rat and Mole were taken into Badger's house, with the bonus that, while Badger, Rat and Mole were sitting cosily by the fire on a level with the audience, one could still see, up above, the Chief Weasel and Weasel Norman keeping their chilly watch in the Wild Wood.

Mark Thompson's costumes incorporated some of the animals' natural appearance – Rat's tail, for instance, and his outsize ears – but not so as to obliterate the actors' human features. Jane Gibson taught the cast the movements of the various creatures they were representing: the linear shufflings of the hedgehogs, the dozy lollopings of the rabbits, the sinuous dartings of the weasels and so on.

Younger actors take to this kind of thing more readily than their seniors. Michael Bryant, playing Badger, was initially sceptical and avoided the movement classes; then in an apparent access of enthusiasm, he asked if he could take home the various videos depicting badger activity. When he came in the next day, he handed back the videos, saying, 'I've studied all these films of the way badgers move, and I've discovered an extraordinary thing: they move exactly like Michael Bryant.' But to most of the actors, some of whom were doubling as different creatures, the animal movement classes were of great value. For example, one could see in David Bamber's Mole that his get-up as an old-fashioned northern schoolboy did not entirely displace the shy, scuttling creature with splayed hands and feet, which people were always after for a waistcoat.

I have tried to do a faithful adaptation of the book while, at the same time, not being sure what a faithful adaptation is. One that remains true to the spirit of the book, most people would say. Well, *The Wind in the Willows* is a lyrical book, and the first casualties, if the book is to work on the stage, were those descriptive passages that give it its lyrical flavour. The splendid music Jeremy Sams wrote helped to compensate for this loss, and his lyrics too – which he dashed off with such speed that I felt, had he had a couple of hours to spare, he could have adapted the whole thing.

Still, the play is nowhere near as gentle and atmospheric as the book. No matter, other people would say, its special charm lies in the characters. But to adapt the text on that principle is not straightforward either, as the tale is very episodic. Rat and Mole disappear for long stretches, as does Badger, and it is not until Toad's adventures get underway that there is anything like a continuous narrative. It was for this reason, I imagine, that A. A. Milne called his adaptation *Toad of Toad Hall*, whereas to many readers of the book, it is Rat and Mole who hold the story together.

The most substantial cut I made had been made by Milne too – namely, the chapter entitled 'Wayfarers All', in which Rat encounters a sea-going cousin. Milne also omitted the mystical chapter 'The Piper at the Gates of Dawn', but this I did include, though I'm not sure what children made of it in the play – or make of it in the book, for that matter. In the play, Pan was heard but not seen, which is just as well: Grahame's description – 'the rippling muscles on the arm that lay across the broad chest . . . the splendid curves of the shaggy limbs disposed in majestic ease on the sward' – makes him sound too much like Mellors the gamekeeper. Both chapters, incorporated into *The Wind in the Willows* at a late stage, recall the kind of pieces Grahame began writing when he worked at the Bank, and which were collected in his first book, *Pagan Papers*.

I ended up making the play the story of a group of friends, with the emphasis on Mole. He is the newcomer who takes us into this world of water and woods and weasels, and whose education is the thread that runs through it all. *The Wind in the Willows* is Mole's *Bildungsroman*. Mole is the only one of the characters I have allowed to have doubts. He doubts if he is having a good time, doubts if he is happy with Rat. He likes Toad as he is, and when the old show-off reforms, it all seems rather dull – have they done the right thing by taking him in hand? Rat and Badger have no doubts, but at the finish, Mole is still wondering.

Jokes apart, the only element in the production that I brought up to date was the Wild Wooders. In the book, they are an occasional presence, but for the play, Nicholas Hytner felt that they should be a constant threat, lurking in the background even at the most idyllic moments, and at one point going so far as to carry off a baby rabbit for their supper – an incident that shocked adults in the audience more than it did children.

In Grahame's day, the Wild Wooders were taken to represent the threat to property posed by the militant proletariat – a view, whatever one's political persuasion, that would be hard to maintain today. Our Wild Wooders ended up as property speculators and estate agents, spivs and ex-bovver-boys, who put Toad Hall through a programme of 'calculated decrepitude' in the hope of depressing its market value. Their plan is to turn it into a nice mix of executive dwellings and office accommodation, shove on a marina and a café or two and market it as the 'Toad Hall Park and Leisure Centre' – 'The horror! The horror!' groans Badger. But the reformed Toad's vision of his ancestral home as a venue for opera, chamber concerts and even actors' one-man shows does not commend itself to Badger either. 'Actors!' he moans, and we know that, before long, he will be loping back to the Wild Wood.

Albert the horse is a nod in the direction of A. A. Milne. Grahame has a horse in the book to pull Toad's caravan, but he does not give him a name or a voice. In *Toad of Toad Hall*, the horse is called Alfred and is a bit of a pedant. I have made him, in another nod to Milne, extremely lugubrious – Eeyore's Wolverhampton cousin. Toad can never remember his name and keeps calling him Alfred, which is not surprising as he is probably remembering him from the other play.

In the blurb written for his publishers, Grahame said that his book was 'clean of the clash of sex'. What this means is that women do not get a look in. There are only three of them to speak of – the washerwoman, the bargewoman and the gaoler's daughter – and only the last is seen in a kindly light. One reviewer of the play described these three as 'coarse human females, coarsely characterized; they seem to come from another production.' No, just from the text, much as Grahame wrote it, where the female sex is generally rubbished. One of the indictments against Toad is that, owing to his car crashes, he has had to spend weeks in hospital 'being ordered about by female nurses'. In addition, he has been 'jeered at, and ignominiously flung in the water – by a woman, too!' Even Toad, who rather fancies the gaoler's daughter, joins in the game. 'You know what *girls* are, ma'am,' he says to the bargewoman. 'Nasty little hussies, that's what *I* call 'em.'

Toad is pretending, but not so Rat, Mole and Badger, all of them confirmed bachelors. Bachelordom is a status that had more respect (and fewer undertones) in Grahame's day than it has now, and certainly he seems to have regarded it as the ideal state from which he had disastrously fallen. Of course, some bachelors are more confirmed than others, and the bachelordoms of Mole, Rat and Badger differ – or I have made them differ. Mole is a bachelor by circumstance, taking his cue from his surroundings. Rat is a single creature and so Mole is happy to be single, too, and set up home with his new friend – though as properly as Morecambe with Wise or Abbott with Costello. But had Mole popped up on that spring morning and found Rat in a cosy family set-up, he could have fitted in there just as well. Judging by the way he makes himself readily at home at Rat's and then at Badger's, Mole is just a natural *ami de maison*.

Rat is solitary by circumstance but also by temperament. He could be played like Field Marshal Montgomery, and as with Monty, there may once have been a great love in his life that he has had to bury. He is certainly a romantic, but his rules and rigidities protect him – have perhaps been devised to protect him – from his own feelings. He's not quite a Crocker-Harris, but certainly a Mr Chips.

Badger has something of the old schoolmaster about him, too. He's less buttoned up than Ratty and because not repressed at all, more innocent. All he gets up to is pinching Mole's cheek and rubbing his little toes – behaviour that was quite commonplace in old gentlemen when I was a boy, when such things were not thought to matter much and were shrugged off by the recipient as just another of the ways that grown-ups were boring.

To fans of the book, even to discuss these well-loved characters in such terms might seem, if not sacrilege, at any rate silly. But an adapter has to ask questions and speculate about the characters in order to make the play work. If presented on stage in the same way as in the book, Rat, Mole and Badger would find it hard to retain an audience's attention because they are so relentlessly nice. Badger is a bit gruff, and Rat can be a little tetchy, but that is as far as it goes; all the faults that make for an interesting character are reserved for Toad.

I felt that the atmosphere of the River Bank had to be less serene, and that, while retaining their innocence and lack of insight into themselves, Rat and Mole – and to a lesser extent – Badger, should be prey to more complicated feelings, particularly jealousy. Thus Mole's arrival on the River Bank to become Rat's new friend is not quite the untroubled idyll it is in the book. It is not long before Mole wants to meet Badger, and of course, he turns out to be a big hit there, too. So now Mole is Badger's friend as well as Rat's, and we go into a routine of 'He's more my friend than he is yours – and anyway, I met him first!' It is a routine children are accustomed to and it is not unknown to grown-ups, particularly in some of life's backwaters – and the River Bank, despite Rat's protestations, can be a bit on the dull side. Newcomers there are eagerly gobbled up, as newcomers always have been in novels of provincial life, from Jane Austen to Barbara Pym.

Toad presents a different problem, and as much for the actor as for the dramatist. It is not that, like Mole and Rat, he is too nice, though Grahame is at pains to emphasize that he *is* nice and, for all his boasting, a good fellow underneath. It is just that we are told before he appears that he is conceited, a show-off and a creature of crazes; then, when he does arrive, he is all these things and goes on being all these things, with none of his disastrous adventures resulting in any disillusionment at all, still less self-knowledge. Finally, and suddenly, at the end of the book he is confronted by the trio of friends and, overnight, becomes a changed character.

Now this is no use to the dramatist at all, and no pushover for the actor either. Characters in a play need to go on a journey, even if it's only from A to B. Mole's journey is a gradual schooling at the hands of Rat in the ways of the River Bank; Rat's journey (in my adaptation) is an emotional schooling at the hands of Mole;

Badger's journey is from solitude to society. But Toad does not go on a journey at all – he goes on his travels, but he does not go on a journey. Until his transformation, he is the same at the end of the book as he is at the beginning; life has taught him nothing.

But unchanging as he is and in defiance of all the rules of drama, children love him, and since Toad has so much of the action, even adults don't mind, until by the end, nobody – adults or children – wants him to change. Nor does he in my version – he just learns to keep it under.

'Keeping it under' is partly what *The Wind in the Willows* is about. There is a Toad in all of us, or certainly in all men, our social acceptability dependent on how much of our Toad we can keep hidden. Mole, by nature shy and humble, has no trouble fitting in; Toad, with neither of these virtues, must learn to counterfeit them before he is accepted. It is one of the useful dishonesties he might have learned at public school (where it is known as 'having the corners knocked off'). Humphrey Carpenter says of Toad that one could imagine him having a brief spell at Eton or Harrow before being expelled – too soon to have learned the social lie that the play teaches him.

TOAD: I say, Ratty, why didn't you tell me before?
RAT: Tell you what?
TOAD: About not showing off, being humble and shy and nice.
RAT: I did tell you.
TOAD: Yes, but what you didn't say was that this way I get more attention than ever. Everybody loves me! It's wonderful!

When I first read the book it seemed to me that Grahame meant Toad to be Jewish. He had endowed him with all the faults that genteel Edwardian anti-semitism attributed to *nouveaux-riches* Jews. He is loud and shows off; he has too much money for his own good and no sense of social responsibility to go with it, and this sense of social responsibility is another lesson he has to learn. The fact that, whenever Grahame has the animals discuss Toad's character, they end up saying what a decent fellow he is underneath it all only seemed to confirm this analysis, and I thought that Grahame must have been thinking of characters like

Sir Ernest Cassel and the Sassoons, the friends and financiers of Edward VII, who moved at the highest levels of society but were still regarded as outsiders. So when I read *The Wind in the Willows* for the BBC, I gave Toad something of a flavour which, if not Jewish, was at least exotic – trying to make his r's sound like Tom Stoppard's, for instance. I expected some criticism for this (not from Tom Stoppard), but none came, and now, having adapted the book for the stage, I am less sure anyway. The text is so full of inconsistencies. Grahame himself may not have known – 'He is and he isn't' as so often the proper answer to such questions.

The nearest Oscar Wilde gets to the River Bank was his remark about ducks. 'You will never be in the best society,' he has a mother say to her ducklings, 'unless you can learn to stand on your heads.' In Toad, there are echoes of Wilde, and not only in his disgrace and imprisonment. Many of Wilde's epigrams would not be out of place at Toad Hall – 'If the lower orders don't set us a good example, what on earth is the use of them?' or 'I live wholly for pleasure; pleasure is the only thing one should live for.' I am not sure that Toad thinks of himself as an artist (though he has been told that he ought to have a salon), but if he did, it would only be as a motorist ('Is motoring an art?' 'The way I do it, yes.') Occasionally he manages an epigram of his own that is worthy of Wilde. 'I have an aunt who is a washerwoman,' says the gaoler's daughter. 'Think no more about it,' replies Toad consolingly. '*I* have several aunts who *ought* to be washerwomen.' But then Toad's gaol cannot have been far from Reading.

At the finish, I have the gaoler's daughter kiss Toad, who does not turn into a prince but straightaway wants Rat to taste the joys of kissing, just as he had once wanted him to share the joys of caravanning. Rat, of course, is reluctant, but finds to his surprise there may be something in this kissing business after all, and generous animal that he is, he wants Mole initiated, too. So the play ends with a hint of new horizons. It is a large departure from the text, of course, where all four of our heroes are left in bachelor bliss, but this alteration is not entirely without justification, echoing as it does the course of Grahame's own life. Courtship and marriage were late joys for him, too, and not such joys either, but that's another story and not one, as I said at the start, that I managed to tell.

My additions and alterations to *The Wind in the Willows* are, I am sure, as revealing of me as the original text is of Grahame. Grahame knew this very well. 'You must please remember,' he wrote:

> that a theme, a thesis, is in most cases little more than a sort of clothes line on which one pegs a string of ideas, quotations, allusions and so on, one's mental undergarments of all shapes and sizes, some possibly fairly new but most rather old and patched; and they dance and sway in the breeze and flap and flutter, or hang limp and lifeless; and some are ordinary enough, and some are of a private and intimate shape, and rather give the owner away, and show up his or her peculiarities. And owing to the invisible clothes line they seem to have some connexion and continuity.

Peculiarities or not, I imagine most writers are gratified that there is an invisible clothes line, if only because it suggests there are things going on in their heads that they are unaware of. Who knows, these unintended recurrences might amount, if not to Significance, then at least to Subtext. The only other piece of mine that has been performed at the National Theatre was my double bill *Single Spies* in 1988. However, it was not until I was adapting *The Wind in the Willows* that I remembered that Guy Burgess, the protagonist of *An Englishman Abroad*, had, in his final rumbustious days at the Washington Embassy, acquired a 12-cylinder Lincoln convertible in which he had frequent mishaps. 'He drove it,' said Lord Greenhill, a fellow diplomat, 'just like Mr Toad.' Poop-poop.

This adaptation was adapted, more than most plays are, in rehearsal, and owes a great deal to Nicholas Hytner, Jeremy Sams and the cast and crew of the original production. I would like to thank them all.

Alan Bennett, January 1991

PART ONE

It is a spring morning on the River Bank and the locals are going about their (not very pressing) business. A troop of rabbits lollops by, followed by a line of hedgehogs, and then come some squirrels. All the River Bank animals seem to patronize the same outfitters, who has kitted them out in a special brand of tweeds that manages to accommodate both tails and ears. Thus the small tails of the rabbits come through their skirts or breeches as do the long plumed tails of the squirrels. The rabbits wear hats that allow their ears free play but the hedgehogs don't wear hats on account of their spiky hair. Some of the squirrel children start scuffling with the young rabbits and a row seems about to break out when everyone's attention is distracted by the sudden eruption, brush in hand, of MOLE.

 MOLE *has close-cropped black hair, a blazer and sandals. He wears NHS spectacles and though he is a mole he could also be an old-fashioned northern schoolboy.*

MOLE: Hang spring cleaning! And hang whitewashing! Oh, the light! The air! The *freedom!*

RABBIT ROBERT: Where do you think you're going? You can't come through here.

MOLE: Why? You don't own the place.

RABBIT ROBERT: I do actually. It'll cost you sixpence.

MOLE: Onion sauce!

RABBIT ROBERT: Don't you onion sauce me. This is private property.

RABBIT ROSE: That's right. You have to pay a toll.

RABBIT ROBERT: At least if you're a mole.

RABBIT ROSE: And haven't stayed in your hole.

MOLE: Well, I won't pay.

RABBIT ROBERT: He won't pay.

RABBIT ROSE: Why won't he pay?

RABBIT ROBERT: Why won't you pay?

MOLE: I've no money . . . bunny.

RABBIT ROBERT: He's no money.

RABBIT ROSE: Oh well . . . we'll overlook it just this once.

RABBIT ROBERT: Yes, particularly since you're new round here . . . but remember, it is private property. Some people. Honestly.

MOLE: Hey, Flopsy.

RABBIT ROBERT: Are you speaking to us?

MOLE: What's this?

RABBIT ROSE: What's what?

MOLE: This. This long . . . sliding . . . gurgling thing?

RABBIT ROSE: What is it? Well, it's a river.

RABBIT ROBERT: Never come across one before, have you?

MOLE: No.

RABBIT ROBERT: So much for onion sauce. The ignorance of some people, honestly.

MOLE: But . . . it's . . . it's wonderful.

RABBIT ROSE: Is it? I've always thought it a bit ordinary.

(MOLE *is still gazing wonderingly at the river when* RAT *rows into view.* RAT, *being something of a sailor, wears a navy-blue blazer and yachting cap. But for his ears, which are rather larger than normal, and the long tail (which he tucks in his pocket) he might be a naval officer who has taken early retirement.*)

RAT: Hello.

MOLE: Hello.

RAT: You're Mole, aren't you?

MOLE: That's right. And you're Rat.

RAT: That's right. How d'you do. Well, this is an unexpected pleasure. A bit far from home, aren't we? Never seen you around here before.

MOLE: No. I've . . . I've taken the day off.

RAT: Taken the day off! I say, that's bold.

MOLE: That's a lovely boat!

RAT: Well, I like it.

MOLE: I've never been in a boat.

RAT: I'm sorry. I thought for a moment you said you'd never been in a boat.

MOLE: I haven't.

RAT: Bless my soul.

MOLE: Why? Is it so nice?

2

RAT: Nice? No, it's not nice. It's the only thing. Believe me, my young friend, there is nothing, absolutely nothing half so much worth doing as simply messing about in boats. In them or out of them, whether you get away or you don't, or whether you never get anywhere at all, there's always something to do, and you're always busy. But *nice* . . . that's not the half of it. Listen, if you've nothing else on this morning what say we drop down the river together and make a day of it?

MOLE: In the boat? Together? Could we? Could we really?

RAT: Certainly. Hop in. Careful. That's it. (*He hands* MOLE *a hamper.*) Put this on your lap.

MOLE: What's in it?

RAT: There's cold chicken in it, cold ham, cold tongue, cold beef, pickled gherkins, sausage rolls, cress sandwiches, ginger beer, lemonade . . .

MOLE: Oh, stop, stop. This is too much.

RAT: Do you really think so? It's only what I always take. The other animals are always saying I'm a mean beast, and cut it very fine. Comfy?

MOLE: Rather.

RAT: Right. Off we go.

MOLE: So this is a river.

RAT: My dear Mole, if I may correct you. Not a river. *The* river.

MOLE: And you really live by the river? What a jolly life.

RAT: By it and with it and on it and in it. It's my world and I don't want any other.

MOLE: Isn't it a bit dull at times?

RAT: Dull?

MOLE: Just you and the river and no one else to chat to . . .

RAT: No one else? My dear fellow, the bank is so crowded nowadays, some people are moving away altogether.

MOLE: What's over there?

RAT: Where?

MOLE: There. That dark place on the horizon.

RAT: Oh . . . nothing.

MOLE: Yes, there is. It's . . . a wood.
    (*He stands up to get a better view.*)

RAT: Don't stand up, you idiot. You'll have the boat over.
(MOLE *sits down again. Pause.*)
Sorry about that. My fault. Shouldn't have called you an idiot. Only Rule One where boats are concerned is 'Never stand up.'

MOLE: Sorry.

RAT: Where were we?

MOLE: You said there was a wood.

RAT: Yes. This looks a good spot. What say we pitch camp here? Steady as she goes. That's it. Make a sailor of you yet. Now, while I lay the tablecloth why don't you unpack the hamper? Peckish?

MOLE: A bit. Well, a lot actually.

RAT: Good. Then don't stand on ceremony. Tuck in.
(MOLE *puts a sandwich in his mouth.*)
Only, Mole. Manners. Napkin first.

MOLE: Oh, sorry. Sorry.

RAT: Allow me. (*He tucks in* MOLE's *napkin.*) Away you go.
(*They start to eat, observed somewhat sceptically by a* HEDGEHOG *and a* RABBIT.)

HEDGEHOG HERBERT: They seem to have clicked.

RABBIT RONALD: The old fellow's probably lonely. Wants a bit of company.

HEDGEHOG HERBERT: Somebody to rabbit on to.

RABBIT RONALD: Do you mind. I find that remark rather offensive.
(RAT, *having finished eating, is taking it easy, but* MOLE (*who hasn't finished eating*) *wanders about still taken up with whatever it is on the horizon.*)

RAT: What is it, old chap?

MOLE: Nothing.

RAT: All right. I'll tell you what it is. It's called the Wild Wood . . . and it's just that we River Bankers don't go there very much.

MOLE: Why? Aren't they nice people?

RAT: We–ell, let's see. The squirrels are all right. And the rabbits, I suppose. Then there's Badger, of course. He's all right. He lives bang in the middle of it, and wouldn't live

4

anywhere else. Dear old Badger. Nobody takes any liberties with him.

MOLE: Why? Who would?

RAT: It's the others, you see . . . the weasels, stoats, and the ferrets. And yet they're all right most of the time. One passes the time of day, 'Morning, Rat,' 'Morning, Weasel' . . . but just occasionally they . . . break out.

(*Hearing themselves talked about the weasels put in a brief appearance. They too have tails and whiskers but in every other respect, camelhair coats, Homburg hats and co-respondent shoes, they are gangsters.*)

Another sausage roll?

MOLE: When? When do they . . . break out?

RAT: Mole. Can I say something? One of the ways we animals have the edge on our human friends and why we're happier than they are is that we don't dwell on possible trouble ahead. Sometimes we need reminding about that, don't we?

MOLE: Sorry, Rat.

RAT: It's a question of manners, really. I find most things are. Apple pie?

MOLE: But, Rat . . .

RAT: Mole, please.

MOLE: . . . but what's beyond the Wild Wood?

RAT: Beyond the Wild Wood comes the Wide World. And that's another topic we avoid. Point taken, Mole?

MOLE: Sorry.

(*Pause.*)

Rat.

RAT: What is it now?

MOLE: I'm not sure this isn't something else I ought not to mention but there are some bubbles in the water.

RAT: Bubbles? O Lord! Clear the food! Quick!

MOLE: Why? What's the matter?

RAT: Too late.

(OTTER, *wearing a striped Victorian bathing suit, has catapulted out of the water and stands in the middle of the picnic, shaking water over everything.*)

OTTER: Hello . . . what's all this? A picnic? Rat, you sly beggar.

5

I don't recall receiving an invitation.

RAT: Because I knew you'd turn up. You never stand on ceremony, though you have stood on Mr Mole's sausage roll.

OTTER: Oh gosh, have I? And we haven't even been introduced.

RAT: Otter, may I present Mr Mole, the wreck of whose sausage roll is now going down your throat.

OTTER: Delighted to make your acquaintance. (*Eating the sausage roll.*) Not wrecked at all. Flavour rather improved I'd say. Is that bloater paste? Splendid!

RAT: Really!

OTTER: Take no notice of Rat. Old comrades in arms, Rat and I. Is he looking after you?

MOLE: I'm having a wonderful time.

(*A small child with goggles and water-wings and a large L on his back struggles up on to the bank.*)

OTTER: This is Portly, my youngest. He's just had his first swimming lesson.

RAT: Well, Portly. What did you think of the water?

PORTLY: Wet, sir.

RAT: Make you hungry, did it? Fancy some potted meat?

PORTLY: Oh yes, sir.

RAT: Well, tuck in, tuck in.

(PORTLY *takes a sandwich.*)

OTTER: What do you say, Portly?

PORTLY: Thank you, sir.

RAT: Who's out on the river today?

OTTER: Who's not out, you mean. Talk about cheek by jowl. Never known the place so crowded. Toad's out for one.

MOLE: Who's Toad?

RAT: Was he in the punt?

OTTER: No. The skiff.

I said to him, Where's the punt?
He said, What punt?
I said, You had a punt.
He said, Did I?
I said, Well I thought you did.
Turns out he'd been showing the punt off to the ducks and ran it over the weir.

6

RAT: The weir?

OTTER: Mind you, he was already getting bored with it. You know Toad.

RAT: It's the houseboat saga all over again.

OTTER: First of all it was sailing . . .

RAT: Then came the houseboat and we all had to go and stay with him on the houseboat . . .

MOLE: Oh, how lovely . . .

RAT: . . . and pretend we liked the houseboat. He was going to spend the rest of his life in a houseboat. It's the same whatever he takes up.

OTTER: He's lucky to have the money to do it.

MOLE: Has he got a lot of money?

OTTER: Toad's a good fellow, I'm not saying that. Just . . . unreliable. (OTTER's *attention has been caught by something on the river.*) We must go. In you get, Portly.

PORTLY: Must I?

OTTER: Yes, and sharpish. Our lunch is rapidly disappearing upstream. (*He somersaults back into the river.*)

PORTLY: Thank you for the potted meat, sir.
(*He holds his nose and nervously jumps in.*)

RAT: Time we were moving on.
(RAT *and* MOLE *pack up.*)

MOLE: His *lunch*? What was the bloater paste?

RAT: Oh, that was just a snack. No. What otters really like are mayflies.

MOLE: Can I row on the way back?

RAT: Not yet, old chap. Have a few lessons first. I tell you, it's not as easy as it looks. Anyway the current's with us, so I'll just let her drift. No rush on the river, you see.
(*They drift back down the river,* RAT *resting on the oars and* MOLE *in the prow.*)
I've never told anyone this before, Mole, but I'm a bit of a poet.

MOLE: Well, I wouldn't worry about it. It's probably just a stage. I once had a shot at the trombone.

RAT: I feel there's a poem waiting to be written about ducks.

MOLE: Ducks?

7

RAT: All along the backwater
    Through the rushes tall
    Ducks are a-dabbling.

MOLE: They're what?

RAT: Dabbling.

MOLE: Oh, I thought you said 'gabbling'. It could be 'gabbling', couldn't it?

RAT: Yes. But I think dabbling's better. Now I've lost my thread.
    All along the backwater
    Through the rushes tall
    Ducks are a-dabbling . . .
    Up tails all.
    Here we are. Home. Watch out!
    (MOLE *gets one foot on the bank and one in the boat, and the boat moves or the bank moves but either way he ends up getting his feet wet.*)
    Oh, you silly creature. Are you wet?

MOLE: Only my foot.

RAT: Well, you'd better come inside and dry off. Look, Mole.
    Not quite sure how to put this but since it's getting late would it be a good idea if you stopped with me for a bit?
    Would you like that?

MOLE: Like it? Oh, Rat. I'd love it.

RAT: Jolly good.
    (RAT'*s house, like his clothes, has a distinctly nautical flavour. It's as much a cabin as a room, with portholes and lots of brass and polished wood; on the wall are a barometer and some ceremonial oars and the seating accommodation is two folding steamer chairs with neat blue cushions.* MOLE *is bowled over.*)
    It's not exactly luxury's lap, I'm afraid.

MOLE: I've never seen such a nice house.

RAT: Yes, well, to tell you the truth, I am rather proud of it. Now here's a towel . . . and don't forget between the toes.

MOLE: Yes, Rat.

RAT: And, Mole.

MOLE: Yes?

RAT: There's no need to keep calling me Rat. It's a bit . . . well . . . formal. My friends call me Ratty. Could you manage

8

that, do you think?

MOLE: Oh yes . . . Ratty . . .

RAT: What about you? Do you have a pet name?

MOLE: I've never had a friend before. My brothers used to call me Moley.

RAT: Moley. I like that. Now pop into bed and then I'll bring you a little smackerel of something.

(RAT *shows* MOLE *his berth in the adjoining cabin and he is bowled over afresh.*)

MOLE: Oh, it's lovely.

RAT: Yes, I think you'll be comfortable. I'll get you a hot brick to warm your toes.

MOLE: Oh, Ratty. It's been a wonderful day.

RAT: It has been nice, hasn't it? Got everything you want?

(*No answer.*)

Good Lord, little chap's asleep. Tired him out. Night night.

(*Now that* MOLE *is asleep* RAT *is free to try out the name of his new friend.*)

Moley.

(*Finding he likes it he nods to himself and puts the light out. As* RAT *and his new friend disappear from view the* HEDGEHOG *and the* RABBIT *pass judgement.*)

HEDGEHOG HERBERT: It won't last, you know. Won't even last the summer.

RABBIT RONALD: Really? Why not?

HEDGEHOG HERBERT: Rat's too prickly.

RABBIT RONALD: You're one to talk.

HEDGEHOG HERBERT: Why?

RABBIT RONALD: You're a hedgehog.

HEDGEHOG HERBERT: Do you mind? I find that remark rather offensive.

Summer has gone and the River Bankers are busy with the autumn harvest as RAT *and* MOLE *stroll towards Toad Hall.*

RAT: Do you write poetry, Moley?

MOLE: You've asked me before, Ratty. No.

RAT: I do. (*To someone passing*) Good morning!

MOLE: How much farther is it to Toad Hall?

9

RAT: Toad Hall? Not far. Do you see this rabbit? The father got
made into a pie last week. (*Very brightly to the* RABBIT) Hello.
As a matter of fact I've just finished a poem today.

MOLE: Is it about ducks?

RAT: How on earth did you know that?

MOLE: I sort of guessed.

RAT: Would you like me to recite it?

MOLE: Would you like to recite it?

RAT: Oh, well, if you insist.

> All along the backwater
> Through the rushes tall,
> Ducks are a-dabbling,
> Up tails all!
>
> Ducks' tails, drakes' tails
> Yellow feet a-quiver,
> Yellow bills all out of sight
> Busy in the river!
>
> Slushy green undergrowth
> Where the roach swim
> Here we keep our larder
> Cool and full and dim.
>
> Everyone for what he likes!
> We like to be
> Heads down, tails up
> Dabbling free!

(*The rabbits and hedgehogs have formed up behind* RAT *and they
take up the chorus as the scene changes and to a burst of English
Heritage music the towers and terraces of Toad Hall rise slowly
into view.*)

ALL: Dabbling free!

> All along the backwater
> Through the rushes tall,
> Ducks are a-dabbling,
> Up tails all!

RAT: And here we are at Toad Hall.

MOLE: My goodness!

RAT: Yes. It really is one of the nicest houses in these parts, though don't say that in front of Toad.

MOLE: Why?

RAT: Toad is a lovely creature and very good-natured but . . . well, he's not very clever and he does tend to be just a trifle boastful.

MOLE: He must be very rich. What does he do?

RAT: Nothing very much. His father was rich, you see, so he doesn't have to earn money, though he's quite good at spending it . . .

(RAT's *enthusiasm tails off as* TOAD *appears. While* TOAD *is dressed like a country gentleman in a loud suit of plus-fours, his green hair and large, round glasses stamp him as a toad.*)

TOAD: Ratty! Good morning. No, don't tell me. This is Mr Mole. We meet at last! How do you do. I'm told you've given the old rascal a new lease of life. And what do you think of my humble home, Mr Mole?

MOLE: It's magnificent.

TOAD: Yes, it's been said that it's the finest house on the whole of the river and, some would say, anywhere else.

(RAT *nudges* MOLE.)

I saw that, Ratty. He's warning you that I show off, Mr Mole. And I do from time to time. But it's only my way. Some people are modest. Some people are not. And I'm not. Why should I be? I've nothing to be modest about. But listen. This is most important. You have to help. Both of you.

RAT: With your rowing, I suppose. Well, you're getting on fairly well, though you still splash a bit . . .

TOAD: Rat, stop. Boating . . . pooh. A footling amusement. I can see it suits you, Rat, but in a curious way I find I've somehow – outgrown it. I've now hit on the real thing – something to which I want to devote the rest of my life. Prepare yourself for a revelation. Shut your eyes.

(*A gypsy caravan is pulled on by* ALBERT, *the horse.*)

Ta-ra!

RAT: Good Lord.

MOLE: Oh, it's beautiful. Ratty, isn't it beautiful!

RAT: (*Drily*) Lovely.

TOAD: That's the real life for you, Rat . . . The open road, the dusty highway – go inside, my young friend – the heath, the common, the hedgerow. Here today and somewhere else tomorrow. Travel, change, interest, excitement.

MOLE: Come in, Ratty. You won't believe it . . . there's little bunks and a cooking stove and lockers and bookshelves, and it's all so snug.

TOAD: I see your young friend is a person of taste, Ratty. Sardines, Mr Mole? You'll find some in the locker. Or a chocolate biscuit? Or both? I promise you nothing whatever has been forgotten. Now I suggest we start off in what . . . half an hour?

MOLE: Oh yes. Yes, please.

RAT: Did I hear you say something about 'we' and 'start'?

TOAD: Now, my dear good old Ratty, don't go all stiff and huffy. You've got to come. You can't mean to stick to your dull old river all your life and just live in a hole in the bank and *boat*?

RAT: Why not?

TOAD: But Rat, Mole . . . I am going to show you the World.

RAT: I do not want to see the World. From what I've seen of it so far it has very little to recommend it. Everybody *doing* things, getting somewhere.

TOAD: You mean the rat race.

RAT: I can't think why they call it *that*. Well, I'm not coming and that's flat. And what's more Mole is not coming either, are you, Mole?

MOLE: No. No, I'm not. Still, it does sound as if it might have been . . . well . . . rather fun.

RAT: No. I belong here.

TOAD: But, Ratty, old chap. I want to show you an England you've only dreamed of . . . the England of heath and common and hedgerow, green roads and ancient tracks. We will camp tonight on the downs, dine off chops, cheese, new bread, freshly churned butter and great swills of beer. And when we've done we'll smoke a pipe and lie gazing up at the quiet stars that have shone down on this England of ours for thousands of years.

RAT: Oh yes . . . yes . . . yes.

TOAD: (*Winking at* MOLE) Never fails.

RAT: Of course, I'm still not keen myself but since Moley clearly wants to go . . .

MOLE: Only if you do, Ratty.

RAT: And it may be I am a bit set in my ways.

TOAD: Excellent. Could you just have a word with the horse? He's being rather tiresome. Meanwhile I'll go and change into my caravanning clothes.

(TOAD *trots off to get into his togs.*)

MOLE: I didn't know there were caravanning clothes.

RAT: Oh, there always have to be clothes for it, else Toad wouldn't want to do it. Now, Albert, what's the matter?

ALBERT: (*Who is a Wolverhampton cousin of Eeyore*) It's Toad. He wants me to pull the caravan and I'm not supposed to pull things. Doctor's orders. When I pull things I pull other things. Like muscles.

MOLE: Oh, Albert.

ALBERT: Now don't start all that stroking. I don't like being stroked. And don't start smacking me on the side of the neck either, still less on the bottom. Smack anybody else on the bottom and it's a punishment, whereas if you're a horse you're supposed to love it.

RAT: Would you like a carrot?

ALBERT: Yes, provided it's in a cream sauce or diced in a little *bouillon*. What I don't want is one of those mucky raw articles. That's another misconception. One carrot and they think you're anybody's. Are you going on this expedition?

MOLE: Oh yes. It'll be fun.

ALBERT: Fun for you. You're not pulling the cart.

(TOAD *emerges in his caravanning outfit and gets on to the box.*)

TOAD: Ready then? Time to go.

ALBERT: Listen, will you talk to me?

MOLE: Of course I'll talk to you.

ALBERT: Toad never does. His conversation is limited to 'Gee up' and 'Whoah!'

13

TOAD: Gee up!

ALBERT: Not my idea of a feast of reason and a flow of soul. Added to which I never get no supper.

RAT: Any supper. I never get any supper.

MOLE: We'll talk to you and give you supper too.

ALBERT: And when I say supper I don't mean one of those nosebag things where you get your kippers all mixed up with the custard.

RAT: Don't you worry.

(MOLE *smacks him on the bottom*.)

ALBERT: There you go again! *Desist*.

(*With* MOLE *holding the horse's head the caravan proceeds on its way to the applause of the rabbits and other well-wishers*.)

ALL: What a lovely caravan!
Isn't she a spanker!

TOAD: Not bad, is she – I can't believe she's all mine!

(*And some not so well-wishers*.)

CHIEF WEASEL: Hello, Toady. Got yourself a horse and cart now?

TOAD: Do you like it?

STOAT CYRIL: What happened to the houseboat?

WEASEL NORMAN: Yeah. And the bike?

WEASEL WILFRED: And the punt?

CHIEF WEASEL: Yeah, your punt, Toady. What happened to that?

TOAD: Such good people. How glad one is to be able to bring a little excitement into their dull lives. Happy, Ratty?

RAT: I am, rather.

TOAD: Who wouldn't be . . . just riding along, taking the world as it comes, meadow giving way to moor and field to forest . . . the scene changing, as change it must, but gently, imperceptibly. That's England, Ratty. England's a caravan. Well! This looks like a good place to camp. Why don't you fellows feed the horse, make a fire and so on. I'd prefer to do all that myself but I've got more serious work to do studying the map and planning the route for tomorrow.

(TOAD *gets into the caravan*.)

RAT: (*To* MOLE) Same old Toad. I say, you rabbits.

A RABBIT: I think he means us.

RAT: You look at a loose end.

ANOTHER RABBIT: Of course we are. We're rabbits.

14

RAT: Why not lend us a hand?

THE SAME RABBIT: I don't know, what do you think?

A DIFFERENT RABBIT: I will if you will.

RAT: Oh, *come on.*

(*The rabbits surprise themselves by buckling to, as do the hedgehogs, helping to make a fire, feed* ALBERT *and fry sausages. In less than no time* RAT, MOLE *and the rest of the company are singing a song around the camp fire where* TOAD (*having spotted that all the work has been done*) *eventually joins them. Attracted less by the singing than the sausages the weasels too come and stand just outside the circle, but what with music having charms to soothe the savage breast, etc., these arboreal ne'er-do-wells are soon singing along with everyone else . . . and the* CHIEF WEASEL *even has to brush away a tear.*)

'Camp Fire Song'

The land of my fathers is a long way away
But I dream every night and I think every day
Of a far-off meadow which is thick with flowers
Which is yours – which is ours.

The land of lost content
The hill of broken dreams
Where swallows whirl in the firmament
And the bright moon beams.

I will go to my fathers when my journey is done
When the world turns to gold in glow of the sun
I will lay me down in the soft sunshine
Which is yours – which is mine.

The land of lost content
The hill of broken dreams
Where swallows whirl in the firmament
And the bright moon beams.

Lyrics by Jeremy Sams

TOAD: This is the life for a gentleman, eh, Rat? Talk about your old river.

RAT: I don't talk about my river, do I, Moley?

MOLE: Not much, no.

RAT: I think about it, though.

MOLE: Ratty.

RAT: What?

MOLE: So do I.

RAT: Time to turn in, I think.

(*During the song a big yellow moon has risen and now it is bedtime.* TOAD *returns to the caravan but thoughtful as ever flings out a couple of blankets for* RAT *and* MOLE *who settle down by the fire.*)

TOAD: Good night, you fellows.

RAT: Good night, Toady.

MOLE: Toad didn't do the washing-up.

RAT: No. He's never done the washing up in his life. He likes the idea of camping but there always has to be somebody to fetch and carry.

MOLE: Us.

RAT: Well, we'll see about that. Good night, Moley.

MOLE: Good night, Ratty. (*Pause; calling*) Good night, Albert.

ALBERT: I was asleep until you said good night.

(*Silence descends on the camp until shadowy figures materialize. All fellow feeling forgotten, it is the weasels.*)

WEASEL NORMAN: This one's Mole, Chief. He'd be no trouble.

CHIEF WEASEL: Yeah, but this is Rat. He's something else.

WEASEL NORMAN: Why not take them all now, Chief?

CHIEF WEASEL: All in good time, Norman. All in good time.

(*The weasels evaporate into the darkness, managing in the process to snaffle from under the nose of its dozy mother a particularly succulent baby rabbit.*

Dawn now breaks, and as the camp and its followers wake up there is a bustle of activity.)

SQUIRREL SHIRLEY: Did you know they lost Florence during the night?

SQUIRREL RAYMOND: No?

SQUIRREL SHIRLEY: Eaten by the weasels.

SQUIRREL RAYMOND: Eaten by weasels? That's terrible. Mind you, I had a shocking night myself.

16

HEDGEHOG HARRY: I don't know what they make such a fuss about the dawn for. I've never been able to go overboard about it.

ALBERT: I don't mind sunrise really. And I don't dislike sunset. It's what's in between depresses me.

(*The caravan is well on its way before there is any sign of its sleeping owner.*)

TOAD: (*Emerging*) Good morning, Ratty. On our way already! What a lovely morning. I could eat a horse.

ALBERT: Oh, could you? Well, I wouldn't say no to some toad-in-the-hole.

RAT: We've had breakfast.

TOAD: Where's mine?

RAT: Oh, it's all eaten. You were asleep.

TOAD: That's rather selfish of you. But don't worry about me. If we pass a likely-looking hostelry I'll partake of something there.

RAT: Well, Toady. I must say I eat my words. I'm really enjoying this.

TOAD: (*Testily*) I'm glad to hear it.

MOLE: Me too.

ALBERT: And I'm not wholly discontented myself.

RAT: The open road. The chequered counties. England spread out in front of us . . .

TOAD: We seem to be going very slowly.

ALBERT: No, we're not. This is what is known as *ambling* and considering it's only nine in the morning some people might think we were going like greased lightning.

TOAD: I can't think why people stare. It's insolent. Those rabbits are even waving. Ignore them, Rat.

RAT: They're just pleased to see us.

TOAD: Can't imagine why. It's just a glorified horse and cart, what's so special about that? And it's so slow, trundling along. Of course that's what this country's like, Rat. England's a caravan. Wants geeing up a bit.

(*There is the sound of a car drawing nearer and a distant poop poop.*)

SQUIRREL SAMUEL: I say, that caravan ought to watch out. There's something coming.

SQUIRREL SHIRLEY: And fast too. Somebody ought to warn them. There could be a nasty accident.

SQUIRREL SAMUEL: A very nasty accident indeed.

(Disaster seems unavoidable but by sheerest chance when the collision occurs both car and caravan are already offstage so the audience is spared the frightful sight of horse-drawn meeting horse-powered and horse-drawn ending up in the ditch. As it is, all we hear is a frightful crash and the sound of a car picking up speed and heading for the horizon while a single cartwheel careers on to the stage as witness to the fate of TOAD'*s once proud caravan.)*

Dear oh dear oh dear. Look at that. I saw that coming, you know.

*(*MOLE *and* RAT *rush on.)*

MOLE: Stop! Come back!

RAT: Villains! Road hogs! *Tourists.* I'll have you in court. You saw that, you were a witness.

(The rabbits to whom RAT *is appealing have of course seen nothing and are already making themselves scarce.)*

MOLE: Ratty. They've gone.

RAT: It's a disgrace!

*(*ALBERT *comes on with a few fragments of cart still attached.)*

ALBERT: That wasn't very nice, was it? Could have been quite dangerous.

*(*TOAD *now staggers on and it is at once evident that he has had a religious experience.)*

TOAD: Poop poop. Poop poop.

RAT: All right, Toady?

TOAD: Ratty. I've had a vision.

ALBERT: Shock. Concussion.

TOAD: There was a great creature . . . like a thunderbolt!

ALBERT: I had a cousin fall in the Grand National, same thing.

TOAD: There was a man in a helmet and he was riding a rainbow, then a cloud of dust and the sound of distant trumpets.

RAT: And the caravan in the ditch.

TOAD: What caravan?

MOLE: Your caravan, Toady. Your pride and joy.

RAT: It's no use, Moley. He's forgotten the caravan already. Caravans, punts, houseboats . . . It's all happened before.

ALBERT: Funny. Without the cart I feel . . . a bit . . . undressed.

TOAD: Rat. You're a man of the world . . . I wonder . . . just out of interest . . . where one would purchase one?

RAT: Purchase what?

TOAD: One of those . . . motor car things.

RAT: Toad, Toad.

TOAD: Poop poop. Poop poop.

RAT: (*Calling after*) Toady! Toady!

> (RAT, *seeing all too clearly what the future has in store, runs after* TOAD, *followed by his friends, whereupon the* WILD WOODERS *run cackling across the stage bearing bits of the looted caravan.*)

Summer has gone and autumn. So now it is winter and RAT *and* MOLE *are taking a brisk walk along the deserted River Bank.*

MOLE: Nobody on the river.

RAT: No. Too cold.

MOLE: Nobody at all.

RAT: There's a duck.

MOLE: Yes.

RAT: Well, that's interesting. I like ducks.

> (MOLE *gives him a pitying look.*)

MOLE: Couldn't we go and see Toad?

RAT: Won't be home. He'll be perambulating the countryside in his latest motor car. That is if he's not smashed it up already.

MOLE: I wouldn't mind going out in a motor car.

RAT: What did you say?

MOLE: Nothing. We could go and see Badger.

RAT: Out of the question. Hates callers. Besides, he lives in the middle of the Wild Wood.

MOLE: You said the Wild Wood was all right.

RAT: So it is. But it's not somewhere we want to go on a cold winter's afternoon.

MOLE: I've never met Badger.

RAT: Once the warmer weather comes I'll introduce you. Though you'll probably find him as dull as you're finding me. I'm off back. Coming?

MOLE: I'll catch you up.

> (RAT *goes whereupon an elegant* FOX *waylays the unsuspecting*

MOLE. *The* FOX, *possibly on the if-you-can't-beat-'em-join-'em principle, is dressed in hunting pink.*)
FOX: Did I hear you mention the Wild Wood?
MOLE: Yes, do you know it?
FOX: One has various elderly female relatives there, largely bed-ridden, alas.
MOLE: I'm sorry.
FOX: They would welcome a visit, a little ray of sunshine like you. That way. Give them my love.

The weasels, the ferrets and the stoats are busy lording it over their territory. This happens to be the Wild Wood but it could be any provincial bus station on a Saturday night. But they are not alone.
CHIEF WEASEL: Mole!
(*The place is suddenly deserted as* MOLE *comes wandering along.*)
MOLE: Well, I don't see what all the fuss is about. It's a bit dark, I admit. But it's only a wood. Somebody might think those trees had faces but I don't. I mean, what is there to be frightened of?
(*But if* MOLE *is as bold as he is pretending to be, why is he saying this out loud? Meanwhile the* WILD WOODERS *flit between the trees and it grows darker.*)
Still, I wish I was back with Ratty round his cosy fireside.
(*Then the whistling begins, and the panting and all sorts of other frightful noises, and* MOLE *begins to panic. He runs this way and that but whichever way he runs he finds his path blocked by one of the* WILD WOODERS.)
CHIEF WEASEL: Well, well, well.
FERRET FRED: Hello, Mole.
FERRET GERALD: How's it going?
STOAT IAN: Lovely weather.
WEASEL NORMAN: Alright, Mole?
STOAT STUART: How's friend Rat then?
WEASEL NORMAN: How's friend Toad?
WEASEL WILFRED: We don't like Toad.
(*The* WILD WOODERS *close in on* MOLE.)
CHIEF WEASEL: A hole is where you belong.

STOAT STUART: Go back to where you belong.

FERRET FRED: We don't like moles who are friends of Toad.

WEASEL NORMAN: We don't like little brown animals.

STOAT IAN: You don't belong in this part of the world.

WEASEL WILFRED: Moles are dirty.

WEASEL NORMAN: Moles smell.

FERRET FRED: Who's a dirty mole then?

(*They begin to chant.*)

WILD WOODERS: We don't like moles. They belong in holes. We
don't like moles. They belong in holes. (*etc*). We don't like
moles. We don't like moles. We don't . . .

(*The* WILD WOODERS *have* MOLE *on the floor now and are
kicking and beating him and the* CHIEF WEASEL *is about to do his
worst and gestures for silence to accentuate the horror when in the
silence is heard a distant but familiar voice.*)

RAT: Moley!

CHIEF WEASEL: It's Rat!

(*The* WILD WOODERS *scatter, only the* CHIEF WEASEL, *who is as
two-faced as they come, runs back with* MOLE's *spectacles.*)

Here's your glasses back, Moley. Only a bit of fun.

RAT: Moley. Where are you? It's me. It's old Rat. Moley.

MOLE: Ratty? Ratty? Is that really you?

RAT: Moley?

(*The* WILD WOODERS *have withdrawn to a respectful distance
but are watching the proceedings, still wondering if they could be in
there with a chance.* RAT, *catching sight of them, puts paid to that
idea.*)

Don't even think about it. Oh thank goodness I've found you,
old chap.

MOLE: Oh, Rat, I've been so frightened, you can't think.
Frightened to death. Oh, oh.

RAT: Hold up, hold up. It's all right. Safe now. Rat's here. You
shouldn't have done it, Moley. We River Bankers hardly ever
come here by ourselves.

MOLE: But why do they do it, Rat?

RAT: It's just their nature. We can't stop here. The weasels are still
somewhere about and it's snowing. Trouble is, I don't quite
know where we are. Up you get, Moley. We must get on.

MOLE: I'm tired out, Ratty.

RAT: Me too, but our only hope is to find some shelter or we're done for. Come on.

(MOLE *trips and falls headlong*.)

MOLE: Oh my leg, my leg.

RAT: What's up?

MOLE: I must have tripped over a tree stump. Oh my, oh my.

RAT: (*Getting out his handkerchief*) No, you didn't.

MOLE: Yes, I did.

RAT: You didn't, Mole. This is a very clean cut. It's not from a tree stump, it's from something sharp.

MOLE: Well, never mind what done it. It hurts just the same whatever done it.

RAT: 'Whatever did it.' Just because we've hurt our leg doesn't mean we can forget our grammar.

(RAT *starts scraping away the snow*.)

MOLE: Hey, Ratty, what about my leg?

RAT: Never mind your leg. Look.

MOLE: So? A doorscraper. What of it?

RAT: What of it? Don't you see what it means, you dull creature?

MOLE: Of course I see what it means. It means that some very careless person has left his doorscraper in the middle of the Wild Wood. And you seem to have forgotten I've hurt my leg.

RAT: Where there's a doorscraper, what else is there?

MOLE: How should I know?

RAT: Well, scrape and you'll find out. There.

MOLE: So? A doormat. What use is that to us? Sometimes, Rat, I don't understand you.

RAT: Yes . . . that's because you're a thick-headed beast. Now dig.

MOLE: I'm not thick-headed. I'm not thick-headed at all. Ratty! A front door!

RAT: You don't say. Now do you understand?

MOLE: It's Mr Badger's.

RAT: Exactly. Pull the bell.

MOLE: You saved us! You saved us!

(MOLE *pulls the bell*. RAT *seizes it from him and yanks it even harder*.)

Oh, Rat, you're wasted here . . . among us simple creatures.

22

You should be at Oxford. Or in the government.

RAT: I'd rather be beside a warm fire. (*He batters on the door.*) Wake up, Badger, wake up. Pull, Mole, pull. We must wake him. Badger, Badger. *Wake up!*

(*There is a sound of many locks being unlocked and bolts drawn and of a gruff voice inside.*)

BADGER: Now the very next time this happens, I shall be very cross. Very cross indeed. Disturbing someone on a night like this. Who is it? Come on, speak up.

RAT: Badger, let us in please. It's me, Rat, and my friend Mole. We're lost.

BADGER: Lost? How can you be lost? You're outside my front door.

(*He opens it.* BADGER *is all dressing-gown. His hair, once black, now has a broad streak of grey down it and though there is a tail somewhere, since he is never out of his dressing-gown we don't see it. His bark, needless to say, is much worse than his bite and his heart melts at the sight of the two friends.*)

Ratty! My dear little man. And it's snowing. I'd no idea . . . and who's this little chap?

RAT: Mr Mole.

BADGER: Mr Mole. But he's colder than you are, Ratty. My dear fellows. Come in. Come inside this minute.

(BADGER *lights the way with his lantern along the passage that goes deep below the Wild Wood into his cosy kitchen. Above ground, where it is not cosy at all, the* CHIEF WEASEL *is beginning to get a little testy.*)

CHIEF WEASEL: That's the second time they've given us the slip. I'm beginning to get cross about this.

WEASEL NORMAN: You see, Chief, that's why I wanted to take them at the caravan.

CHIEF WEASEL: Norman.

WEASEL NORMAN: Yes, Chief?

CHIEF WEASEL: A word of advice. Never say I told you so.

WEASEL NORMAN: Why, Chief?

CHIEF WEASEL: Because it gets right up my nose.

(*Meanwhile back in* BADGER's *house* RAT *and* MOLE *are getting into dressing-gowns in front of the fire.*)

BADGER: You shouldn't be out on a night like this, little chaps
like you. But I've got a grand fire going . . . your little
friend's shivering, Ratty.

RAT: Well, we both are.

BADGER: But look at his face. I bet your little toes are like ice . . .

MOLE: Oh, thank you, Mr Badger.

RAT: It was his own fault.

BADGER: No, Ratty. None of that. You've had a narrow escape.
What's this, have you hurt yourself? Ratty, your little
friend's hurt himself.

RAT: I know.

(*It's fairly plain by now that most of* BADGER's *attention is
concentrated on* MOLE *and this makes* RAT *somewhat tetchy.*)

BADGER: How did you come to do that?

MOLE: On the doorscraper.

BADGER: On *my* doorscraper? Oh dear. How come you let him do
that, Ratty?

RAT: The truth is, Badger, Mr Mole has been a bit of a scamp.

MOLE: I have, yes.

BADGER: Well, he's young, you see, Rat. They get ideas into their
heads. Look at that face. So cold. Here we are.

(*He binds up* MOLE's *leg.*)

RAT: He would go off on his own. Wouldn't be told.

BADGER: Sense of adventure, was it? I understand that – I'm the
same. Rat's more cautious, you see. But you won't do it
again, will you, Master Mole.

MOLE: No. Never.

BADGER: Do you hear that, Ratty? He won't do it again. Now
what's wanted is a bowl of piping hot soup. And I've got just
the thing on the hob. (*He gets* MOLE *a bowl.*) A bowl for
Mole. Poetry, eh Rat, your province.

RAT: Shall I get my own?

BADGER: Oh yes, you help yourself. Feeling better now, are we?
Warmth coming back into those little toes of yours?

MOLE: Yes thank you, Mr Badger.

BADGER: Goodness me, *you* musn't call me *Mr* Badger. No, no.
My friends call me . . . Badger.

MOLE: My friends call me Moley.

BADGER: Do they?

RAT: Badger's too old for nicknames. He'd probably be happier calling you Mole.

BADGER: Rat knows best as always. Anyway, tell me what's been happening in your part of the world. How's friend Toad getting on?

RAT: Another smash-up last week and this time a bad one. He will insist on driving himself and he can't do it for toffee.

BADGER: What he wants is a chauffeur.

RAT: Exactly. I said to him, 'Get a steady, well-trained animal . . . a hedgehog for instance; they're very good on the road.'

BADGER: How many has he had?

RAT: Smashes or machines? Oh well, it's the same thing with Toad. This is his seventh.

MOLE: He's been in hospital three times and he's paid out a fortune in fines.

BADGER: Has he, Moley? Dear me.

RAT: And that's part of the trouble. Toad's well off, we all know, but he's not a millionaire. Bankrupt or killed, it's going to happen sooner or later, unless . . .

BADGER: Unless you and me take him in hand.

RAT: Quite.

BADGER: Of course, you understand that I can't do anything right now.

RAT: Oh yes. Of course. (*Pause.*) Why not?

BADGER: Winter. I never do anything much in the winter. But it's a different thing once it gets to spring . . . One starts to get more bounce . . . Do you feel that in the spring, Moley?

MOLE: Oh yes.

BADGER: Well, I know I do . . . but that's decided; as soon as it gets to spring the first item on the agenda is for you, me and Mole to take Toad seriously in hand. Now, you're going to have to snuggle down in these chairs if that's all right.

(*It's all right with* MOLE *because* BADGER *has installed him in a big comfy armchair.* RAT *on the other hand has been allotted an upright dining chair that is not comfy at all. Nor does he do any better when* BADGER *comes to allocate the bedding.*)

So. Here's a blanket for Rat and a nice quilt for Mole. Just this once we'll skip brushing our teeth. That's it. Little toes warm, are they?

MOLE: Oh yes thank you, Badger.

BADGER: Good, good. You comfortable, Rat?

RAT: I'm all right.

BADGER: Night night.

MOLE: Night, Badger.

(BADGER *retires*.)

RAT: Do you like old Badger?

MOLE: Oh yes.

RAT: Not too fierce for you?

MOLE: Fierce? I thought he was very kind.

RAT: He is kind.

MOLE: And understanding.

RAT: Of course that comes with age, you see he's much older than you or me.

MOLE: He didn't seem old to me.

RAT: Oh, he is . . . how old exactly would you say Badger was, Moley?

(*There is no answer from* MOLE, *who has the quilt over his head*.)

Moley? Oh. Little fellow's asleep. Seems old to me, Badger.

(*Outside in the Wild Wood* WEASEL NORMAN *is still managing to strike the wrong note*.)

WEASEL NORMAN: Of course, Chief, if I'd bitten their heads off when I wanted to we could have been fast asleep by now.

CHIEF WEASEL: Norman.

WEASEL NORMAN: Yes, Chief?

CHIEF WEASEL: Do you know what it's like to have your head bitten off?

WEASEL NORMAN: Come again, Chief?

CHIEF WEASEL: Want to find out?

WEASEL NORMAN: Sorry, Chief.

Next morning finds BADGER *serving some very adhesive porridge to two small hedgehogs,* TOMMY *and* BILLY.

BADGER: One spoonful for Tommy.

HEDGEHOG TOMMY: Oh, thank you, sir.

BADGER: And another spoonful for Billy.

26

HEDGEHOG TOMMY: Say thank you.

HEDGEHOG BILLY: Thank you, sir.

BADGER: I'm just going into my study to . . . to catch up on my correspondence.

(*We see* BADGER *go into his study, settle down in his chair with a handkerchief over his face.*)

HEDGEHOG BILLY: (*Pulling a face*) It's not like Mum's porridge.

HEDGEHOG TOMMY: I know, but we mustn't leave any.

(RAT, *who has plainly had a less than comfortable night, edges painfully off his dining chair.* MOLE *has slept much better of course, and not only because he has been in the comfortable chair but because being underground suits him.*)

(*Standing up and pulling* HEDGEHOG BILLY *to his feet*) Good morning, sir.

RAT: As you were, as you were. Where's Mr Badger?

HEDGEHOG TOMMY: The master's gone into his study, sir, to catch up on his correspondence.

RAT: And what brings you here?

HEDGEHOG TOMMY: We were trying to find our way to school . . . and we lost ourselves in the snow, sir.

MOLE: Hello, Tommy. Hello, Billy.

(*There is a ring at the doorbell.*)

RAT: The door, Tommy. Off you go.

HEDGEHOG BILLY: Look, Mr Mole.

(HEDGEHOG BILLY *demonstrates to an interested* MOLE *how Badger's porridge clings to the spoon even when held upside down.*)

RAT: Don't toy with your food, Billy.

(OTTER *plunges into the room, scattering snow everywhere.*)

OTTER: Hello, Ratty, you old fraud.

RAT: Get off, Otter, you're wet through.

OTTER: You ungrateful beast. Of course I'm wet through. You'd be wet through if you'd been battling through the snow. How's friend Mole? Still in one piece? I don't know what all the fuss is about.

RAT: What fuss?

OTTER: Where's Badger?

HEDGEHOG TOMMY: The master's gone into his study to catch up on his correspondence . . .

RAT: What fuss?

OTTER: Having a little nap, is he?

HEDGEHOG TOMMY: No, sir. He's gone into his study to catch up on his correspondence.

OTTER: You not eating that porridge?

HEDGEHOG BILLY: No, sir.

OTTER: Ungrateful little devil.

(OTTER *swallows it at one go.*)

RAT: Otter. What fuss?

OTTER: Your disappearance. Your presumed demise. That fuss. I was just taking a little stroll along the river bank yesterday when I came upon these ducks and they said, They've gone. I said, Who?

They said, Rat.

I said, Rat?

They said, Yes.

I said, Why?

They said, Mole.

And I look round and blow me if there isn't a search party dragging the weir. So I thought I'd come over to the Wild Wood and sniff around a bit and have a word with Badger.

RAT: Thanks, Otter.

OTTER: Where is Badger?

HEDGEHOG TOMMY: The master's gone into his study . . .

OTTER *and* RAT: Oh, shut up.

HEDGEHOG TOMMY: (*Continuing*) . . . to catch up on his correspondence.

OTTER: Is nobody going to offer me some breakfast?

(BADGER *enters.*)

BADGER: What's all this din? Oh, I might have known. Hello, Otter.

OTTER: Sorry, Badger. Did I disturb you?

BADGER: No. No. I was just catching up on my correspondence.

(HEDGEHOGS TOMMY *and* BILLY, *proved right at last, put out their tongues, so* OTTER *clouts them.*)

Ah. How's my little Mole this morning? Did you sleep?

MOLE: I did. Even better than at Ratty's.

28

RAT: Oh. Thank you.

BADGER: Rat, why don't you help Otter to some breakfast? Off you go, you hedgehogs. I see you've eaten all your porridge. Won't want any dinner today. Now go straight home.

(RAT *takes* OTTER *upstage to give him some breakfast and with his rival safely out of the way* BADGER *interrogates his new friend.*)

How do you get on with Ratty?

MOLE: Very well. We're great friends.

BADGER: Keep you in order, does he?

MOLE: Well . . .

BADGER: Right way and a wrong way?

MOLE: A bit, but I don't mind.

BADGER: That's because you're like me . . . down to earth. Trouble with Ratty is that he can sometimes get a bit . . . well, ratty. Ha ha.

RAT: What's that?

MOLE: Nothing, Ratty.

(*Redoubled laughter from* BADGER.)

RAT: Can't we all share it? I wish I could find something to laugh at. It seems to me we're in a spot. Now, Otter, you've got your ear to the ground. What's the feeling in the Wild Wood?

OTTER: They are all up in arms about Toad, Badger. They could break out at any time.

RAT: Just what I was saying last night. It's why, come the spring, we've got to do something about Toad.

BADGER: Why wait for the spring?

RAT: I beg your pardon? You said . . .

BADGER: I know what I said. I said spring. And it isn't spring, but the curious thing is I feel it's spring. I've got that spring feeling.

RAT: (*Uncertainly*) Have you? Oh. Good.

MOLE: Me too.

BADGER: Good. So. The hour has come.

OTTER: Whose hour?

BADGER: Toad's hour. Now, are we all ready . . . no, Ratty, leave the washing-up. Now. We don't want to upset the Wild Wooders more than we have to, so we won't go out by the front door.

RAT: What other way is there?

BADGER: Lots of ways. I'm sure Moley's house is the same. (*To* MOLE) Move that table. I've got a secret entrance that takes us right to the edge of the wood. The weasels won't even know we've gone.

(BADGER *moves the horn of a gramophone and a door opens in the wall.*)

So, Otter. A lantern for you. And, Moley, if you'll take my hand and, Rat, you bring up the rear. Next stop, Toad Hall. (*They disappear down the passage leaving* RAT, *who looks around a little sadly.*)

(*Calling*) Come along, Rat. Keep up with Mole and me. Don't dawdle.

RAT: Sorry.

Unaware that his character is about to be forcibly improved, TOAD *is at the wheel of his latest motor car, leading an admiring throng of* RABBITS *and* HEDGEHOGS *in a lap of honour around Toad Hall.*

TOAD: (*Singing*) The army all saluted
    As they marched along the road.
    Was it the King? Or General French?

RABBITS: No. It was Mr Toad.

TOAD: The Queen and her ladies-in-waiting
    Sat in the window and sewed.
    She cried, 'Who is that handsome man?'

RABBITS: They answered, 'Mr Toad.'

(BADGER, RAT *and* MOLE *march sternly on.*)

TOAD: Hello, you fellows. Just the people I want to see. How do you like her? Isn't she a beauty? And she goes like a bird. I can't wait to get her on the road. Pile in and I'll show you. What's the matter? Why these long faces?

BADGER: Rat. Mole.

(RAT *and* MOLE *seize* TOAD *and bundle him away – though* MOLE (*and it is to his credit*) *finds this a more difficult duty than does* RAT.)

TOAD: Get off, you fellows. What are you doing? Help! Leggo! You can't frogmarch me, I'm a Toad.

BADGER: Are you the car salesman?

SALESMAN: I am. Parkinson's the name. Mr Toad is one of our

most valued customers.

BADGER: I bet he is. Well, Mr Toad has changed his mind. He will not require the car. The craze is over.

SALESMAN: Motor cars is not a craze, sir. They are the coming thing. Motor cars is progress, sir. Motor cars is the future.

BADGER: Not for toads. Good morning, Mr Parkinson.

(MR PARKINSON, *who is not used to having his customers kidnapped, goes off in a huff and the new motor car with* TOAD, *who has given his captors the slip, running frantically in pursuit.*)

TOAD: Stop, stop, where is he going? Where is he taking my beautiful motor?

BADGER: Back.

TOAD: Back? How dare you?

BADGER: Toad. Listen to me. You are suffering from an illness.

TOAD: Rubbish. I never felt better in my life. Oh, my beautiful motor.

BADGER: A mania. A sickness of the mind.

TOAD: Poop poop.

RAT: Don't be rude, Toad.

TOAD: Rude? May I remind you you're on my property?

BADGER: If you are to recover from this illness it will depend on your being kept away from the source of the infection. Motor cars.

TOAD: Motor cars are not an infection. Motor cars are my life.

RAT: But these crashes, Toad. The fines. The Wild Wooders think you've got money to burn.

TOAD: So? One can't help being rich. The Wild Wooders don't scare me.

MOLE: Hear hear! I think Toad should stand up to them.

RAT: Shut up, Mole. You don't understand this.

BADGER: You're quite right, Moley. Toad should stand up to them. But he should also mend his ways. Keep his nose clean. Eschew motor cars.

TOAD: What?

BADGER: Give them up. Toad, old friend. I want you to solemnly promise never to touch another motor car.

TOAD: Certainly not. On the contrary I solemnly promise that the very first motor car I see, far from eschewing it, poop poop, I shall go off in it.

BADGER: Very well, Toad. You bad low animal. Since you won't yield to persuasion, we'll see what force can do. Take off those ridiculous clothes.

TOAD: Shan't. Shan't. Shan't.

BADGER: Take them off him, you two.

TOAD: This is an outrage. Stop it, you idiots. Ow! You're hurting me.

(RAT *and* MOLE *start taking* TOAD's *togs off, though again* RAT *is notably more zealous about it than* MOLE.)

BADGER: You knew it must come to this in the end.

TOAD: Didn't.

RAT: Yes, you did.

TOAD: Didn't. Didn't. Didn't.

BADGER: You've squandered all your father's money.

TOAD: Haven't. Got loads left. Anyway buying motor cars isn't squandering. It's . . .

BADGER: It's what? An investment?

TOAD: It's fun. Moley. You're a young person. You understand.

MOLE: It's better this way, Toady, honestly.

BADGER: Make him put on some proper clothes and send these to the jumble sale.

TOAD: A jumble sale? My lovely togs! Oh!

(TOAD *begins to weep and* MOLE, *ever the soft-hearted one, seeks reassurance from* BADGER.)

MOLE: It is better, isn't it, Badger?

RAT: Of course it is.

BADGER: But it's going to take time. Days, weeks even.

Some time has passed, long enough anyway for there to have been a jumble sale because some hedgehogs trundle on, unsuitably dressed in the choicer items of TOAD's *motoring gear.* TOAD *has meanwhile decided that any wheels are better than none and comes on in a bathchair with poor old* RAT *doing the pushing.*

HEDGEHOG HAROLD: How is Mr Toad? How is his car-itis?

RAT: Still refusing to walk, I'm afraid.

TOAD: (*Weakly*) That's my coat. Ratty. He's wearing my coat.

HEDGEHOG HAROLD: Yes! I look rather a dog in it, don't you think?

TOAD: Take it off! Take it off this minute. You're not fit to wear it.

RAT: Toad. Behave. I think you'd better go.

HEDGEHOG HAROLD: (*Shaking his head*) Tragic. Tragic.

(TOAD *sinks back in his chair, seemingly on his last legs, but no sooner is* RAT's *back turned than he seizes the controls of the bathchair and drives it like a mad thing. However, when* RAT *turns back to him he is once more the touching invalid.*)

RAT: (*To* TOAD) You all right?

(MOLE *and* BADGER *come in together and the fact they are together is all that is needed to make* RATTY . . . *well, ratty.*)

MOLE: There you are, Ratty . . . I thought I'd have a little trip out with Badger if it's all right with you.

RAT: (*Huffily*) Oh. It's all right with me. Feel free. I'm surprised you even bother to mention it. But, Moley. Put your muffler on.

(MOLE *goes – though probably not to put on his muffler.*)

BADGER: Moley's such good company. Of course, we've got a lot in common.

RAT: Yes.

BADGER: But Rat . . . watch him.

RAT: Watch who?

BADGER: Toad.

RAT: Of course I'll watch Toad. I wasn't born yesterday.

MOLE: (*Off*) Badger!

BADGER: Coming, Moley.

(BADGER *goes off, chuckling.*)

RAT: Watch Toad! Honestly. How are you feeling today, old chap?

TOAD: So kind of you to ask. Kindness itself. But never mind me. How are you? And how's your little friend Mole?

RAT: Oh, little friend Mole's all right. Little friend Mole's on top of the world.

TOAD: You've been so good to him, Ratty.

RAT: I have.

TOAD: Taught him everything you know.

RAT: Quite.

TOAD: And now he's gone off with Badger.

33

RAT: Only for the afternoon.

TOAD: Oh, of course.

(TOAD *you see, though a fool in all sorts of ways, still knows more about the heart than* RAT *does.*)

Mole's not ungrateful, Ratty . . . just young.

RAT: If you bucked up, Toady, we could take a little stroll ourselves.

TOAD: Dear Rat. How little you realize my condition. 'Take a little stroll.' If only I could. How I hate being a burden to my friends, but I shan't be one much longer now.

RAT: I'm glad to hear it. We could go up the river.

TOAD: Dear simple Ratty. I shall be going up the river all too soon.

RAT: That's good news!

TOAD: Ratty, I just wondered . . . it's probably too late already but could you fetch me . . . a doctor?

RAT: Why, you're not ill, old chap?

TOAD: Ill? Not really. I just know, as we animals do know, that I have come to the end of some kind of road.

RAT: Nonsense, Toady. Of course I'll fetch a doctor if you want one, but I'm sure he'd just say you needed a tonic.

TOAD: A tonic. If it were only that. Is it getting dark? Has the sun gone in?

RAT: No.

TOAD: It seems dark to me. Ratty . . .

RAT: Toady, let go of my arm . . .

TOAD: Listen, Ratty. Forget the doctor. Fetch me a lawyer.

RAT: A lawyer?

TOAD: Quickly, Ratty. I have many responsibilities.

RAT: Yes, yes, of course. But, Toady, let go of my arm. Badger should have told me how bad it was, Mole too. But they don't care. I'm the only one who cares. Toady. Toady. Can you hear me?

TOAD: Are you the lawyer? Take this down. This is the Last Will and Testament of Toad . . .

RAT: No, Toady, it's still me, Ratty.

TOAD: Haven't you gone yet? It's so dark . . . I want the sun. Give me the sun, Ratty, give me the sun!

RAT: Toady . . . Toady.

TOAD: What?

RAT: Hang on. Please hang on.

(*He rushes away and there is silence for a moment before from the huddled heap in the chair we hear:*)

TOAD: (*Singing*) The clever men at Oxford
    Know all that there is to be knowed,
    But none of them know one half as much
    As wonderful Mr Toad.

I could have been an actor, I suppose, though it's no job for someone of my intelligence. 'Is it getting dark?' Brilliant. I was quite moved. Not that it takes much to fool Rat. I mean, he's a worthy fellow with many good qualities but very little in the intelligence department. As in due course Badger will doubtless tell him. Ha ha! They're all such children. They think I'm a fool but sometimes I feel I'm the only one who's really grown up.

TOAD *sets off down the road. He can walk but he is so rich he normally doesn't need to, so while it would not be true to say he is hitch-hiking he is certainly on the look-out for any likely-looking motor vehicle. This being a story it is not long before there is the sound of a motor horn (poop poop) and a splendid car draws up beside him. Two goggled* MOTORISTS *alight.*

RUPERT: Well, how do you like her, Monica?

MONICA: Like her, Rupert, I love her!

RUPERT: Peckish?

MONICA: I'll say. This motoring lark really gives a girl an appetite.

RUPERT: What say we adjourn to yonder hostelry, see what mine host can do in the way of fodder?

MONICA: What a topping idea!

RUPERT: Give the old girl time to cool off.

(*They adjourn, leaving* TOAD *transfixed by the car*.)

TOAD: I know this car. It's the one Badger had taken away. I suppose there's no harm in just sitting in her. No one could possibly object to that, could they? I suppose it would be very naughty to take her for a little ride. No. You're quite

right, it would be wicked. Just a teeny little ride even?
No.
Still, I wonder if she starts easily.
Goodness!
Well, now she's started I'll just run her a few yards. It's bad for the engine if you don't.
Oh my! Oh my!
(TOAD, *having started the engine, releases the handbrake, depresses the clutch, puts the car in gear and, gently easing his foot off the clutch and giving a touch on the accelerator, he slowly moves off. Purists and driving instructors will have noted that he has omitted to check his driving mirror and to give the signal for 'I am moving off' but after all this is the first motor car he has driven for several months so it is an exciting moment. It is so exciting in fact that he soon throws caution to the winds, goes faster and faster until suddenly (and possibly avoiding a hedgehog) he drives into a pond. Fans of Racine and Corneille will again be relieved to learn this takes place offstage, but one thing leading to another, the next scene takes place in a magistrate's court.*)

MAGISTRATE: I understand that the prisoner is a member of the middle classes and has a charming home in a riverside setting, parts of which date back to the fourteenth century.
CLERK: The riverside setting?
MAGISTRATE: No, stupid. The charming home. Moreover, he regularly sits down to meals of at least five courses, besides which, and one might think that this is the clincher, he doesn't have to do his own washing-up. Is that right?
TOAD: Quite right. I've never done the washing-up in my life.
MAGISTRATE: I'm glad to hear it. In short, the prisoner is generally agreed to be a man of such modesty and delicate sensibility that he would be an ornament to any prison in which he were to find himself. That is one side of the picture . . . the other need not detain us long. The prisoner has been accused of taking and driving away a motor car, apropos of which I'd just like to ask the court one question. Why should the prisoner steal a motor car when he can, as we have heard, just as easily buy one?

CHIEF WEASEL: Why should he buy one when he can just as easily steal one?

MAGISTRATE: I hadn't thought of that. Are you a witness?

CHIEF WEASEL: No, your honour. Just a weasel with the public interest at heart.

MAGISTRATE: Now the prisoner is alleged to have driven the car into a pond. Tell me, have you ever driven into a pond before?

TOAD: No, your honour.

MAGISTRATE: So this is a first offence?

FERRET FRED: He's driven into a haystack.

MAGISTRATE: Really? Who are you? Identify yourself.

FERRET FRED: I'm just a ferret who cares for justice, your honour.

MAGISTRATE: Well, a haystack and a pond are a very different kettle of fish, so I'm going to ignore that.

STOAT STUART: He had a close shave with a cow, your honour.

MAGISTRATE: Dear oh dear. And who are you?

STOAT STUART: A stoat who knows the difference between right and wrong, your honour.

MAGISTRATE: I don't like the sound of a close shave with a cow.

CLERK: Is the cow in court, your honour?

MAGISTRATE: I don't know. Is the cow in court?

(*There is an awkward pause until the* CHIEF WEASEL *nudges* WEASEL NORMAN, *and though he is hardly a cow look-alike he dutifully stands up.*)

WEASEL NORMAN: Yes, your honour.

RAT: That's not a cow, your honour. It's a weasel.

WEASEL NORMAN: I'm a cow.

RAT: You are a weasel.

WEASEL NORMAN: I'm not. Moo.

(*There is pandemonium in the court, shouts of 'Cow!' 'Cow!' and counter-cries of 'Weasel!' 'Weasel!'*)

MAGISTRATE: Stop it, stop it. Whether the witness is a cow or a weasel might exercise an Oxford philosopher but it need not detain us here.

FOX: Sir, sir.

MAGISTRATE: Oh, I'm fed up with being interrupted. What is it?

FOX: The prisoner's driving brought a hen of my acquaintance to the brink of nervous collapse. She didn't know whether she was coming or going.

MAGISTRATE: Hens never do know whether they're coming or going.

FOX: This one did. She was very single-minded. Only now she's lost her head completely.

MAGISTRATE: And who are you?

FOX: I'm a fox with a conscience.

BADGER: Rubbish!

MAGISTRATE: I don't want to hear any more. Despite all these objections I still retain the favourable impression I had of the prisoner when he first stepped into the dock. I keep thinking of that riverside mansion, where, who knows, I might one day be a guest . . .

(TOAD *has begun to doze off and it takes a poke from* RAT *to alert him to the benefits that might accrue from an offer of hospitality.*)

TOAD: Oh yes. Any time you please. It will be a pleasure.

MAGISTRATE: Oh, that's very kind of you . . . though that does not affect my judgment in the least. Do you do kedgeree for breakfast at all?

TOAD: Oh yes. And devilled kidneys.

MAGISTRATE: Oh, my favourite. However, kedgeree and kidneys to one side, my inclination is to let the prisoner go free. With one small proviso, namely the prisoner must never under any circumstances go near a motor car again. He must never ever drive.

CLERK: What do you say to that?

TOAD: (*Very subdued*) Never.

MAGISTRATE: Excellent. Case dismissed.

TOAD: No. Stop.

I don't mean I never will.

I mean I never won't.

MAGISTRATE: You never won't what?

TOAD: I never won't . . . not drive. I love motor cars. Motoring is my destiny! Petrol runs in my blood. I was born to drive. Poop poop. Poop poop.

(*He starts driving the dock and there is uproar in the court.*)

SHOUTS: Seize him.
Restrain him.
Put him in neutral.

BADGER: He is not himself, your honour.
RAT: The trial has turned his head.
TOAD: (*Together*) No, it hasn't. Poop poop.
MOLE: Believe me, your honour, he's very nice underneath.

TOAD: I am Toad, the King of the Road. Out of my way, out of my way.

MAGISTRATE: Seize him, somebody. Now that the prisoner has revealed himself in his true colours, the only difficulty that presents itself is how we can make it sufficiently hot for the incorrigible rogue and hardened criminal now cowering in the dock before us.

FERRET: Objection, your honour. He isn't cowering.

(*The* CHIEF WEASEL *gives* TOAD *a rabbit punch. I think this is all right; cf. The Englishman gave her a French kiss, or, The cat dogged his every footstep.*)

CHIEF WEASEL: He is now.

MAGISTRATE: Thank you. That was very public-spirited of you. Prisoner at the bar, you have been found guilty on the clearest evidence of stealing a valuable motor car. What is the stiffest penalty we can impose for this offence?

(*The* WILD WOODERS *all hold up nooses.*)

CLERK: Twelve months, which is lenient.

MAGISTRATE: Oh, I was hoping to pass a much longer sentence.

TOAD: Well you can't, Big Nose.

MAGISTRATE: What did the prisoner say?

CLERK: Big nose, your honour.

MAGISTRATE: Do I have a big nose?

CLERK: Not especially.

MAGISTRATE: So it's not fair comment.

CLERK: No. Cheek.

MAGISTRATE: Can I give him anything for that?

CLERK: Oh yes. Twenty years.

MAGISTRATE: Jolly good. That's cheered me up no end. Twenty years. Take him down.

(*As he struggles with the ushers and policemen the valiant* TOAD
*– and at this low point in his fortunes he is valiant – still
continues to sing his song.*)

TOAD: The world has held great heroes
    As history books have showed
    But never a name to go down to fame
    Compared with Mr Toad.

    Poop poop.
    (*The policemen hit him with their truncheons.*)

MOLE: Don't hurt him. Oh, Ratty. They're hurting him.

RAT: No, no. They're policemen. They don't hurt people.

MOLE: Oh, Toady.

TOAD: Moley, Ratty, Badger. My friends. Help me. Help me.
    (TOAD *is led away between the jeering ranks of weasels, ferrets
and stoats, but as he is hauled past* BADGER *this gentlemen
solemnly raises his hat – a literary reference which is likely to pass
unnoticed. In the downfall and trial of* TOAD *Kenneth Grahame
was probably thinking of Wilde's trial. When Wilde was led
away after being sentenced his friend Robert Ross was seen to
raise his hat. There are great clankings of doors, turning of keys
and dripping of walls as* TOAD *is taken down into the depths of
the castle where Toad's* GUARD *rouses the ancient* GAOLER.)

GUARD: Odds bodikins. Rouse thee, old loon, and take over from
us this vile Toad, a criminal of deepest guilt and matchless
artfulness and resource. Watch and ward him with all thy
skill and mark thee well, greybeard, should ought untoward
befall, thy old head shall answer for his . . . and a murrain on
both of them.
    (*'Come again?' would be a proper response to this but the*
GAOLER *is long past repartee and just takes* TOAD *and locks him
in a dungeon.*)

Meanwhile BADGER, RAT *and* MOLE *make their melancholy way
home.*

BADGER: The parting of the ways. You're sure you won't come
and stay?
    (MOLE *looks at* RAT.)
    You're very welcome.

RAT: No. We'll get on home.

BADGER: Sad day. Not going to be much of a Christmas. Goodbye Moley, little chap. Safe journey.

(BADGER *disappears into the Wild Wood as* RAT *and* MOLE *go on in the direction of the River Bank.* RAT, *though, seems nervous and keeps looking over his shoulder.*)

MOLE: He was brave, Toad, singing his song in the court.

RAT: Very foolish, if you ask me. He should have kept his mouth shut.

MOLE: At least he went down fighting.

RAT: Yes. Silly fellow.

MOLE: You're always so sensible, Rat. I can't bear to think of him stuck in some dark damp hole.

RAT: No. It's no place for a toad.

(*Somewhere there is an unkind laugh and not for the first time* RAT *feels someone is in the shadows watching them.*)

Time enough to worry about Toad when we're safely home. Come along.

MOLE: What's the matter, Ratty?

RAT: Nothing. I just have the feeling we're being watched. You see as soon as the word gets back about Toad the Wild Wooders are going to start celebrating.

(RAT *has been moving ahead quickly but* MOLE *has stopped.*)

MOLE: Ratty. Come back. I want you quick.

RAT: Oh come along, Mole, for goodness' sake.

MOLE: It's my home. It must be quite close.

(RAT *hasn't heard.*)

RAT: Can't stop now, old chap. Must press on.

MOLE: But Ratty –

RAT: Listen, Mole, we can't hang about. It's late and I'm not sure we're alone. Be sensible.

(MOLE *runs after* RAT *then suddenly starts crying.*)

RAT: Anything wrong?

MOLE: I know it's a shabby little place and not as smart as yours . . . but I was fond of it.

RAT: Fond of what?

MOLE: I just wanted to have one little look, only you wouldn't turn back. Oh, Ratty, it was *home*.

41

(RAT *stops.*)

RAT: I'm a beast. A thorough beast.

MOLE: No, no.

RAT: My best friend eating his heart out and what do I do? Tell him to pick his feet up. Rat, you're a fool. You don't see what's under your nose. So. Now we've got that straightened out, it's about turn.

(RAT *heads back.*)

MOLE: We can't. What about the Wild Wooders?

RAT: Hang the Wild Wooders. We're going to find your little house. Come on. You're in charge now.

MOLE: It's too late and too dark. I shouldn't have said anything.

RAT: Now whereabouts was it . . . about here, I think.

(MOLE *begins to sniff.*)

MOLE: Yes, yes. Mmm. Mmmmmm.

(*Suddenly* MOLE *disappears, or as suddenly as he can when he has to open a trapdoor in the stage.*)

RAT: Mole. Mole. Where are you?

MOLE: (*Out of vision*) Here.

(RAT *disappears too and as the scene changes we find them both coming down the stairs at Mole End.*)

Outside the front door is a little gravelled forecourt (not to say patio) with on one side a garden seat, flanked by a roller and some ferns, with on the other a skittle alley. For the National Theatre production Mark Thompson managed to contrive most of the delights of Mole End but this rather Pooterish pleasaunce had to be omitted. RAT *therefore comes directly into* MOLE's *dusty front room where* MOLE *shows off his two Staffordshire figures.*

MOLE: That's Garibaldi.

RAT: Was he a mole?

MOLE: No. He was a hero of modern Italy. That's Queen Victoria.

RAT: Was she a hero of modern Italy?

MOLE: No. Though she could have been if she'd wanted to be. It's not a patch on your place, Ratty.

RAT: Nonsense, old chap. I'm sure it's absolutely . . . delightful.

MOLE: Oh, Ratty. Why ever did I do it?

42

RAT: Do what, old fellow?

MOLE: Bring you to this poor cold little place when you might have been at River Bank toasting your toes before a blazing fire.

RAT: Absolute nonsense. What a capital place! So . . . compact. So labour-saving. Oh, Mole, I congratulate you. It's perfect.

MOLE: Do you really think so?

RAT: The stove's laid already so we'll soon have the place warm. Meanwhile, Moley, why don't you find yourself a cloth and have a little dust around?

MOLE: Do you like this bunk under the stairs? That was my idea.

RAT: I like it all, Moley. It's so . . . *cosy.* Oh, what's the matter now?

(*It is cold, it is dusty and here still are the evidences of the spring cleaning abandoned on that memorable morning so long ago. Still,* RAT's *making the best of things cheers up his friend until another thought strikes him and he slumps on his bed in despair.*)

MOLE: Food. I've nothing to give you for supper. Not a crumb.

RAT: Really? Well, what's this? A sardine opener. If there's an opener there must also be the wherewithal that's to be opened. Namely a tin of sardines. (*And to no one's surprise he finds one.*) And what's this? A German sausage? A biscuit tin containing . . . surprise, surprise . . . biscuits. And what have you got here? Mole, you dark horse, beer. It's a banquet!

(*As they prepare to eat there is the sound of small feet outside. Still on watch for the weasels,* RAT *is straightaway on the alert.*) What's that?

(*The sound of 'Ding dong merrily on high' answers his question.*)

MOLE: No, no. It's only the fieldmice. They've come carol singing; they always come to Mole End last of all.

RAT: Come on. Let's have a look at you.

(RAT *opens the front door but the fieldmice flood in through every door in the room, form up and, conducted by* MOLE, *finish their carol.*)

FIELDMICE: Ding dong merrily on high
     In heaven the bells are ringing.
     Ding dong verily the sky

Is riven with angels singing:
Gloria
Hosanna in excelsis.

MOUSE MARK: We've missed you, Mr Mole.

MOLE: I've missed you.

MOUSE MAUREEN: Don't you live here any more?

MOLE: I live on the River Bank with Mr Rat, though I still keep
this on as a . . . *pied à terre*.

MOUSE MALCOLM: Who looks after you?

MOLE: We look after ourselves.

MOUSE MARTIN: Who cooks?

MOLE: Mr Rat cooks.

MOUSE MARGARET: Don't you have a mother to look after you?

MOLE: No.

MICE MARTHA *and* MARY: We do.

MOLE: I did once.

MOUSE MALCOLM: What happened to her?

RAT: Here, what are all these questions?

MOLE: You mustn't mind. They're always like this.

MOUSE MAUREEN: Did you have a mother, Mr Rat?

RAT: Once upon a time. Not now.

MOUSE MARK: Are you an orphan?

RAT: Certainly not.

MOUSE MARGARET: No mother? Who puts the top back on your
toothpaste?

MOUSE MARK: Who airs your vest?

RAT: We fend for ourselves. We're bachelors.

MOUSE MAUREEN: Is that nice?

RAT: It's the only thing.

MOLE: Look what I've found. A tin of toffees. Now off you go.
Merry Christmas.
(*To calls of 'Merry Christmas' the mice go off but form up again
outside.*)

RAT: Well, I don't know about you, Moley, but I'm ready to
drop. Sleep is simply not the word. That your bed? Well, I'll
take the bunk. What a ripping house this is. Everything so
handy.
(*They get into their separate beds, just this once not brushing their*

44

teeth again and though nobody has turned down the lamp the lights begin to dim, and we hear another carol begin outside.)

MOLE: Ratty.

RAT: What?

MOLE: It's lovely to be home again but I don't really want to live here any more. I don't want to leave River Bank.

RAT: No? I thought you might.

MOLE: It's nice to see all my things again but I'm happy the way we are.

RAT: Moley.

MOLE: Yes, Ratty.

RAT: Thanks, old chap.

(*As we rejoin the world above we see that snow has begun to fall and the fieldmice, unlike the normal run of carol singers, have decided to do a second stint, joined by the whole cast, even the weasels, though since they aren't wearing their hats and overcoats they don't look nearly as menacing. Together they sing the first verse of 'In the Bleak Midwinter' as the lights fade.*)

ALL: In the bleak midwinter,
Frosty winds made moan,
Earth stood hard as iron,
Water like a stone.
Snow had fallen,
Snow on snow.
In the bleak midwinter
Long ago.

PART TWO

These days a prisoner of TOAD's *social position and financial resources could expect to be sent directly to an open prison, but* TOAD's *prison is anything but open. He has the dungeon to himself, it's true, but* TOAD *is not at the moment disposed to look on the positive side. Dressed in the traditional prison garb of overalls printed with broad (green) arrows he sits on his little bench contemplating his lot with no equanimity at all. Were there a psychiatrist attached to this gaol he would diagnose* TOAD *as 'subject to violent mood swings'.*

TOAD: Poor Toad. Poor little Toady. All aloney. On his owney. Nobody wants him. Nobody cares. I had a big house once. Servants. Friends. Wise old Badger. Clever intelligent Rat. Sensible little Mole. Why did I not listen to you? O foolish, foolish Toad. It's the end of everything. At least it's the end of Toad which comes to the same thing. Thrust into this dark, damp dungeon, despised by the world, deserted by his friends, whom he entertained entirely at his own expense. Ungrateful Badger. Sanctimonious Rat. Silly Mole. Where are they when I need them? All nice and snug at home while I'm stuck here for twenty years. I can't bear it . . . *twenty years!* Oh, it's not *fair.* (*He goes into a paroxysm of grief, kicking his legs and banging his fists on the ground.*

    There is a shaft of light as the GAOLER'S DAUGHTER *comes in with a plate.*)

GAOLER'S DAUGHTER: Dinner.

TOAD: Dinner? *Dinner!* At a time like this? I couldn't. (*Pause.*) What is it?

GAOLER'S DAUGHTER: Bubble and squeak.

TOAD: Bubble. And squeak. How insensitive people are. No. No. Never.

GAOLER'S DAUGHTER: I'll take it away then.

TOAD: (*Hastily*) *No.* I might just manage to force down a mouthful. After all, I owe it to my friends.
    (*Snuffling, he takes a mouthful or two.*)

46

GAOLER'S DAUGHTER: You like that?

TOAD: Not particularly.

GAOLER'S DAUGHTER: Oh well.
(*She makes to take it away again.*)

TOAD: No. I mean I don't dislike it. It's perfectly acceptable, in its way. Only, it's not what I'm used to at Toad Hall.

GAOLER'S DAUGHTER: What are you used to? Tell me about Toad Hall.

TOAD: Toad Hall is a self-contained gentleman's residence in a picturesque riverside setting. It is very unique in its way and though parts of it date back to the fourteenth century it has up-to-the-minute sanitation and the last word in billiard rooms.

GAOLER'S DAUGHTER: Bless the animal. I don't want to *rent it* . . . just tell me something about it. Tell me about the linen cupboards.

TOAD: The linen cupboards? Well . . . naturally I've never been in them. I imagine they are stacked with piles of snowy white sheets, immaculately pressed pillow slips and big thick towels galore.

GAOLER'S DAUGHTER: It sounds paradise.

TOAD: Toad Hall? (*Airily*) No. Just a well-run gentleman's residence.

GAOLER'S DAUGHTER: I wish I could see it, Toady. (When all's said and done he is rather a pet.)

TOAD: I wish I could take you there, my dear. (She's a comely enough lass, though the idea that a toad out of the top drawer should throw himself away on a mere skivvy is frankly ludicrous.)
(*They cuddle.*)
Who knows? Perhaps one day I can find you a position below stairs.
(*They uncuddle smartish.*)

GAOLER'S DAUGHTER: Below stairs? You're a convict. You're in here for twenty years.

TOAD: I was forgetting. Twenty years! Twenty years!

GAOLER'S DAUGHTER: There, there. I'm a fool to myself, I know, but I've got a real soft spot for you.

TOAD: I know. So many people do.
  (*He blows his nose vigorously and while he doesn't quite examine the results, it's still a bit off-putting.*)
  It's known as charm.
GAOLER'S DAUGHTER: I just wish I could think of a way of getting you out of here.
  (*There is a distant call, echoing down the prison corridors:* WASHING! BRING OUT YOUR WASHING!)
  Here comes my aunt. She's a washerwoman.
TOAD: Think no more about it. I have several aunts who ought to be washerwomen.
  (*The call gets closer:* WASHING! PUT OUT YOUR WASHING!)
GAOLER'S DAUGHTER: She washes for all the convicts in the castle.
TOAD: How lovely for her . . . all those terrible vests and big men's smalls.
  (*The* WASHERWOMAN *comes into the dungeon.*)
GAOLER'S DAUGHTER: (*Thoughtfully*) Actually, you're not unlike one another . . .
TOAD: I beg your pardon?
GAOLER'S DAUGHTER: (*Still thoughtful*) Only she can come and go as she pleases . . .
TOAD: Lucky her.
  (*You can see what's coming and I know it's no business of mine but prisoners in plays and operas so often escape by getting round gaolers' daughters that you'd think daughterlessness would have long ago become part of the job specification.*)
GAOLER'S DAUGHTER: (*Decisively*) Listen, Toad. You're very rich and Aunty's very poor.
TOAD: That's the way the world is, I'm afraid. Aunty is doubtless carefree and happy whereas we rich are burdened with our responsibilities. I myself am on the board of several companies . . .
GAOLER'S DAUGHTER: What I mean, silly, is that if you made it worth her while, she might lend you her clothes and you could escape disguised as her. Aunty!
TOAD: Me dress up as a washerwoman? What a distasteful idea!

(*But the* GAOLER'S DAUGHTER *is already explaining her plan to* AUNTY.)

I say, couldn't I be a lady novelist . . . or a high-born prison visitor? I mean *her*?

WASHERWOMAN: Him? I don't see the likeness at all.

GAOLER'S DAUGHTER: (*Mouthing*) Give her some money.

TOAD: What?

(TOAD, *never quick on the uptake where self-preservation is concerned, doesn't immediately twig. The* GAOLER'S DAUGHTER *mimes bribery.*)

Oh yes, sorry.

WASHERWOMAN: I do begin to see a distant resemblance.

(*More money changes hands.*)

Oh yes. Come to think of it we could be sisters.

GAOLER'S DAUGHTER: Now, Aunty – the first thing is to change your clothes.

WASHERWOMAN: What for? It's not Friday.

TOAD: The disguise, madam.

GAOLER'S DAUGHTER: Undress.

WASHERWOMAN: Here? I'm a married woman.

TOAD: Are you stupid or something? You've had your money.

WASHERWOMAN: Oh yes. That's it, isn't it! You've been paid. Now take your clothes off! Very well, but only to my bloomers. A line's got to be drawn somewhere.

(*She begins to undress – an awesome sight.*)

TOAD: Believe me, madam, this is far more distressing for me than it is for you. They're so smelly.

WASHERWOMAN: I wash other people's clothes. I'm not paid to wash my own.

GAOLER'S DAUGHTER: Now we'll tie you up.

WASHERWOMAN: Tied up? You didn't say anything about being tied up.

TOAD: Let me. She's a strong woman but they'll imagine I overpowered her. No mean feat for someone weakened by months of close confinement and virtual starvation. I'll sit on her first.

WASHERWOMAN: Get off me.

(*She sends* TOAD *flying.*)

49

GAOLER'S DAUGHTER: Aunty, you've been paid, behave.

WASHERWOMAN: I don't care. The nasty little blighter, I'll . . .

TOAD: That's enough out of you, madam.

(*Toad puts a laundry bag over the* WASHERWOMAN's *head, which puts paid to further argument.*)

GAOLER'S DAUGHTER: Now, Toad. Put the dress on. You'll make a very good woman.

TOAD: Yes. I'm not unattractive . . . though I'm not sure this is really my colour.

GAOLER'S DAUGHTER: You look just the ticket. Aunty, stop moaning.

(*A furious grunt.*)

I don't think it will be difficult to get past the guard. My aunt is a woman of unblemished reputation and a keen Methodist and the guard is sure to keep his distance.

TOAD: What do you mean – keep his distance?

GAOLER'S DAUGHTER: Well, you know men. So good luck, little toad, and if you get back to your nice house remember the humble gaoler's daughter who took a fancy to you.

TOAD: I shall. I shall. Perhaps when I open the house to ordinary people, you can come over for tea. Bye bye, Aunty.

(*The sack lunges blindly at* TOAD *but happily misses.*)

This is a far far better thing you do than you ever did before.

(TOAD *must have got past the warders outside the castle because the next time we see him he is trying to sidle past the* GUARD *at the gate.*)

GUARD: Well, if it isn't Bouncing Betty, how are we today?

TOAD: Nicely thank you, how are you?

GUARD: Oh, we're very demure. Now, I've a bone to pick with you.

TOAD: What sort of bone?

GUARD: Last week I was short of a sock and missing a jersey.

TOAD: If you don't put that hand back where it belongs you'll be missing more than a jersey. Keen Methodist indeed! Open this gate and look sharp about it.

GUARD: You've changed your tune.

TOAD: Yes, and you'd better change yours or you'll feel my hand.

GUARD: I have felt it. It's all scaly.

50

TOAD: That's because I've been up since five o'clock this morning rinsing your vests. Men! What it must be to be a woman! Life a constant struggle with the opposite sex! Though I suppose I've only myself to blame. Where looks are concerned I beat most women into a cocked hat! But now I must make a beeline for home where I can get out of this malodorous frock. And how convenient! Here's a train.

(*A train pulls up beside him.*)

TRAIN DRIVER: Hello, mother, you don't look very happy.

TOAD: Oh sir, I am a poor washerwoman who's lost all her money and can't get home.

TRAIN DRIVER: Dear me. And you've got kiddies waiting for you, I dare say.

TOAD: Nine of them. At least. There may be more, only they never keep still long enough for me to count them. And they'll be hungry and playing with matches and getting their little heads stuck fast in the railings. Oh dear oh dear.

TRAIN DRIVER: Tell me, do you wash a good shirt?

TOAD: Shirts are my speciality. Shirts are to me, sir, what daffodils is to Wordsworth.

(*And deprivation was to Philip Larkin.*)

TRAIN DRIVER: Well, I'll tell you what I'll do. I go through a power of shirts in this job. So if you'll wash me a few when you get home I'll give you a ride on the engine.

TOAD: Oh, sir, thank you, sir.

TRAIN DRIVER: Hop on.

TOAD: Well, I won't hop on. If I *hopped* on somebody might think I was a frog or something of that kind. The idea! Ha ha! There we are.

TRAIN DRIVER: Comfy? Off we go.

(*There is a rush of steam, the sound of wheels, a whistle and the train is off.*)

TOAD: Oh, isn't this exciting . . . the fields, the trees, the world flying past. This is the way to travel! Tell me, Mr Engine Driver, how much would an engine like this cost?

TRAIN DRIVER: Cost? You're not thinking of buying one?

TOAD: Me, a poor washerwoman, how could I?

TRAIN DRIVER: You'd have to wash a deal of shirts before you saved up for one of these. I say, that's unusual, the signal's against us.

(*We see a signal fall and as the train screeches to a halt the* TRAIN DRIVER *gets down and presses his ear to the ground. He peers back the way they have come.*)

Funny. We're the last train running in this direction tonight and yet I could swear we're being followed.

TOAD: Followed?

TRAIN DRIVER: Yes. By another train. I'm sure of it.

TOAD: Well, let's get on then.

TRAIN DRIVER: No, no. I can't go against the signal. I can see it now, there is another train. It's full of people. Ancient warders, policemen and shabbily dressed men in bowler-hats, obvious and unmistakable plain-clothes men even at this distance, and all of them shouting, 'Stop, stop!'

DISTANT CRIES: Stop, stop!

TOAD: Go, go! Oh please go.

TRAIN DRIVER: Washerwoman, have you been telling me the truth?

TOAD: Yes. No. Oh, save me, dear kind Mr Engine Driver. I am not the kindly simple attractive laundress that I seem to be. I am a toad . . . the well-known and popular Mr Toad, of Toad Hall in the County of Berkshire. I have only this afternoon escaped from a noisome dungeon into which, should that train catch up with us, I shall shortly be thrust again. Let me fling myself on your mercy, kind engine driver . . .

TRAIN DRIVER: Here, steady on. What were you in prison for?

TOAD: Borrowing a motor car.

TRAIN DRIVER: I don't hold with motor cars.

TOAD: Nor do I.

TRAIN DRIVER: There's too many of them for my money.

TOAD: I do so agree.

TRAIN DRIVER: Railways not roads is my motto.

TOAD: My sentiments exactly.

TRAIN DRIVER: Doubtless these people following us are all outraged motorists.

TOAD: Yes. Sports-car drivers, horn sounders, people who flash headlights . . .

TRAIN DRIVER: Representatives of the AA and the RAC and the Road Hauliers' Federation and others of their vile breed. Well, Toad, I ain't going to be the one to hand you over to the four-wheeled fraternity. So listen carefully. I'm going to turn my back and when I turn round again you will, to my utter surprise, have jumped off the train and disappeared. You understand me?

TOAD: Oh yes.

(*The* TRAIN DRIVER *turns his back, only* TOAD, *who hasn't understood him, is still there.*)

TRAIN DRIVER: I said, 'I'm going to turn my back and when I turn round again you will, to my utter surprise . . .'

TOAD: Oh, sorry.

(*He jumps down. The signal changes and the engine steams off.*)

TRAIN DRIVER: Toodloo, Toad. Now I'm going to lead them a right dance.

(*The* TRAIN DRIVER *reverses his engine and goes back to meet the oncoming train. There is a sound of two massive engines grinding to a halt and then a moment later motorists, ticket collector, policeman and warders rush on pursued by the crazed train-loving* ENGINE DRIVER *wielding an axe. When he has chased them all from the stage* TOAD *slowly raises his head and finds himself looking up into the inquiring face of* ALBERT.)

ALBERT: Hello, Toad.

TOAD: I beg your pardon?

ALBERT: I said, 'Hello, Toad.'

TOAD: Toad? I'm a washerwoman.

ALBERT: Yes, and I'm Sherlock Holmes. It's not another one of your crazes, is it? Caravans, cars and now dressing up in women's clothing.

TOAD: Ssh. This is my disguise.

ALBERT: Well, I've penetrated it.

TOAD: Who are you?

ALBERT: You don't recognize me? I'm not in disguise. I'm one of your ex-employees. Albert.

TOAD: Albert, of course. My trusty steed. My long-lost friend.

ALBERT: Cue for bottom-smacking.

(TOAD *smacks his bottom.*)

TOAD: What are you doing here?

ALBERT: After the caravan incident my doctor advised me to seek employment in a less as it were stressful occupation, and preferably one where motor cars didn't come up behind me and without so much as a by-your-leave biff me on the bottom. Hence the barge now coming slowly round the bend. The large lady is the barge lady, my new employer. Virginia Woolf she isn't, but her pie and peas is to cooking what Michelangelo was to ceiling painting. I will introduce you.

TOAD: No, no. She mustn't know we know each other. There, there, old fellow.

(*He starts smacking* ALBERT's *bottom.*)

ALBERT: (*Under his breath*) Don't *do* that.

BARGEWOMAN: Nice morning, ma'am.

TOAD: Is it? Not for a poor washerwoman who this very morning got a letter from her married daughter telling her to drop everything and come at once. Are you a mother, ma'am?

BARGEWOMAN: I was once. Where was this married daughter of yours living, ma'am?

TOAD: Near the river, ma'am, not far from an elegant self-contained gentleman's residence called Toad Hall. Perhaps you've heard of it.

BARGEWOMAN: Toad Hall? I certainly have. And it just so happens I'm headed that way myself. Hop on the barge. One more don't make no difference to Albert.

ALBERT: Oh no. And why draw the line at one? One washerwoman doesn't make no difference . . . why not offer a lift to the entire staff of the Snow White Laundry? Plus their dependent relatives. Albert doesn't mind. The more the merrier.

BARGEWOMAN: He's cheered up. He was very depressed this morning. So, you're in the washing line, ma'am?

TOAD: Yes. One is a career woman, for one's sins. I cater for all the gentry, which means one gets a respectable type of undergarment which in this business is half the battle.

BARGEWOMAN: You don't do all that work yourself, ma'am?

TOAD: Oh, I have girls . . . twenty or so. But you know what girls are; all trollops.

BARGEWOMAN: Are you *very* fond of washing?

TOAD: I love it. Love it. It's my vocation. Laundry is my life!

BARGEWOMAN: Well, what a blessing it is that I met you. We can both do each other a good turn.

TOAD: (*Nervously*) In what way, precisely?

BARGEWOMAN: I like washing too. However I've made the mistake of marrying this idle specimen who never does a hand's turn. He's off with the dog now, seeing if he can't pick up a rabbit for dinner, leaving me stuck with the steering and how do I get on with my washing?

TOAD: Oh, forget the washing. Fix your mind on that rabbit . . .

BARGEWOMAN: Rabbit? How can you think about rabbit when there's such a treat in store?

TOAD: What treat?

BARGEWOMAN: Why, my washing, silly, a whole heap of my scanties and whatnot.
(*She gets him his tub, washboard and a packet of Rinso soapflakes.*)
There you are . . . the tools of your trade. The raw materials of your art.

TOAD: Well, I suppose any fool can wash. To a person of my intelligence it will be a pushover.

BARGEWOMAN: I bet you can't wait. Smell those! My hubby's socks. Then there's some coms, this heavy-duty liberty bodice, three soiled corsets . . . oh and look at these (*a pair of bloomers*) . . it's a laundress's banquet.

TOAD: I don't feel very well.
(TOAD *starts to rinse and scrub with no great enthusiasm and a great deal of slopping the water about and general mess, while at the same time getting tied up in the stuff that he's washing and gradually getting furiouser and furiouser.*)

BARGEWOMAN: (*Singing*) Happy to float
In a lazy old boat
On a lovely sunny day.
Drifting along,

Singing a song
Wash all your troubles away
Completely. Happy to glide
As you go with the tide,
As you wend your weary way,
Drifting along
As you're singing a song
On this lovely sunny day.

(*This traditional ballad from the pen of Mr Jeremy Sams comes to an abrupt end when* TOAD *hangs the washboard on the line rather than the washing, a departure from established laundry procedure that convinces the* BARGEWOMAN *of something she has suspected for some time.*)

Here. I've been watching you. You're never a washerwoman. I bet you've never washed so much as a dishcloth all your life.

TOAD: Don't take that tone with me, madam. Washerwoman? No, I am not a washerwoman. I am Toad, the well-known and distinguished Toad, the landed proprietor. I'm under a bit of a cloud at present but I'm still streets ahead of you . . . a common bargewoman.

BARGEWOMAN: A toad? Why, so you are. Ugh. A horrid, crawling toad, and in my nice clean barge too. Now that's something I will not have.
(*She grabs hold of* TOAD *and thrusts him overboard.*)
Over you go! And good riddance! Ugh, what a nasty scaly hand.

TOAD: Did you see that? Did you see it?

ALBERT: Why, laundry person, I see you're wet through! (Notice how I'm keeping up your disguise.)

TOAD: There's no need to, stupid. She's twigged that I'm a toad.

ALBERT: I'm not surprised. You never took me in for a minute.
(TOAD *starts undoing* ALBERT's *harness.*)
Here, what're you doing?

TOAD: I'm riding you back to Toad Hall.

ALBERT: You can't do that.

BARGEWOMAN: Stop that. Stop that this minute.

ALBERT: I've got a bad back. Besides I'm quite happy here. My only complaint is that it lacks a bit of civilization.

BARGEWOMAN: Albert. It's a toad. That washerwoman is a toad.
(*Now that* ALBERT *is out of harness the barge naturally begins to drift, so the* BARGEWOMAN *has to leap for the bank and grab the tow rope herself. Meanwhile* TOAD *tries unsuccessfully to mount the horse.*)

TOAD: I'll give you civilization. I'll give you as much civilization as you want.

ALBERT: Can I have the run of the library?

TOAD: Yes, yes.

ALBERT: And you won't object if I put my nose in a book?

TOAD: No.

ALBERT: Because I like a bit of Tennyson now and again.

TOAD: She's got out of the barge.

BARGEWOMAN: Listen, you horrible toad. That horse is my property.

ALBERT: Property? I'm not your property. I'm not anybody's property. You'd better get on, Toady. Her property indeed. All property is theft.
(*They gallop off and the* BARGEWOMAN, *unable to follow because she is still tethered to her tow rope, promptly bursts into tears. Two young rabbits come innocently along trailed by the* CHIEF WEASEL *and* WEASEL NORMAN. *Suddenly the two weasels bring out bags of sweets which they offer to the rabbits, who, very sensibly, scream in terror and take to their heels. Only then does the* CHIEF WEASEL *notice the blubbering* BARGEWOMAN.)

CHIEF WEASEL: The good lady seems a trifle upset. Perhaps you should inquire why. And, Norman . . . sensitively.

WEASEL NORMAN: Hello, darling. Why the waterworks?

BARGEWOMAN: I haven't got anybody to pull my barge.

WEASEL NORMAN: Come again, my love.

BARGEWOMAN: I've been robbed.

WEASEL NORMAN: The stupid cow's been robbed, Chief.

CHIEF WEASEL: Who by, Norman?

WEASEL NORMAN: Who by, my little slice of suet pudding?

BARGEWOMAN: A toad – he stole my horse.

WEASEL NORMAN: A likely story. A toad stealing a horse . . . a toad! A toad, Chief! You don't think . . . ?

CHIEF WEASEL: Just ask her which way it went, Norman.
BARGEWOMAN: That way.
CHIEF WEASEL: Thank you, madam.
(*They rush off after* TOAD.)

Having eluded their pursuers TOAD *and* ALBERT *come upon a* GYPSY *eating stew from a pan.*

TOAD: Can you smell something?
ALBERT: Well, it's not me.
TOAD: Stew. I smell stew. Good evening, Mr Romany.
GYPSY: Good evening, washerwoman.
TOAD: That looks a lovely stew. I could do with some stew.
GYPSY: Want to sell that there horse of yours?
TOAD: What? Me sell this beautiful young horse of mine? Oh no.
    It's out of the question. This is a blood horse. His brother-in-
    law ran in the Grand National.
GYPSY: Then why is he delivering washing?
TOAD: (*Confidentially*) Nerves.
ALBERT: Nerves?
TOAD: He's highly strung . . . which is what makes him such a
    goer.
GYPSY: Shilling a leg.
TOAD: A shilling a leg. Ah.
ALBERT: What're you up to?
TOAD: Shut up, I'm counting.
    (TOAD *counts the legs.*)
    It appears to come to two, but I think it should come to four,
    but I could never think of accepting only four shillings for a
    horse like this.
ALBERT: I should think not.
TOAD: Keep quiet.
GYPSY: Five . . . and that's three and six more than it's worth.
ALBERT: It's a scandal.
TOAD: Ssh. I have a plan. Look here, gypsy. This is my final
    offer: six and six cash down plus as much stew as I can
    possibly eat in that pot. It's a Prize Hackney.
GYPSY: It's a wicked price. All right.
    (TOAD *is given his stew while the* GYPSY *examines* ALBERT'*s*

58

teeth, smacks his bottom, etc. TOAD *pats* ALBERT.)

TOAD: Goodbye, old friend.

ALBERT: *Goodbye?* I thought you said you had a plan.

TOAD: Yes, that was it. Six and six and as much stew as I could possibly eat.

ALBERT: But what about me?

TOAD: Albert. You will have to stop thinking about yourself all the time. It creates a very unfortunate impression. Goodbye.

ALBERT: Toad!

TOAD: Don't work too hard.

ALBERT: Why did I let Toad take me in? I was happy pulling the barge. I was happy in my meadow at Toad Hall. Now I shall have to plod round back streets and pull a rag-and-bone cart for the rest of my days, never more to gallop in green fields.

GYPSY: Come on, you.

(*The* GYPSY *hauls him away.*)

It seems a long time since we were on the River Bank but things don't appear to have changed, and we find RAT *and* MOLE *taking their evening stroll.*

MOLE: It's not the same, is it?

RAT: What?

MOLE: Without Toad?

RAT: Oh, Toad.

MOLE: That's who you're thinking about, isn't it? Haven't spoken all evening.

RAT: As a matter of fact it isn't. Though I suppose it's time we trekked over to prison to pay him a visit. No, I was thinking about Otter.

MOLE: Otter?

RAT: I dropped in there today. Mole, I'm afraid they're in trouble. Little Portly's missing again.

MOLE: Well, he's always getting lost. He'll turn up . . . Otter hasn't an enemy in the world.

RAT: No enemies? Hunters, with their long poles and those shameful dogs. Anglers. Gamekeepers.

MOLE: In our world, I meant, Ratty. Everybody likes the otters, even the weasels, and Portly's such a pet.

RAT: Yes, but it's been days now. And Portly hasn't learned to swim very well. Otter's worried about the weir.

MOLE: The weir?

RAT: The current's so strong he wouldn't stand a chance.

MOLE: Oh dear.

RAT: I suppose we ought to think about turning in.

MOLE: No. I should never sleep. Let's paddle upstream. The moon's coming up and at least it's better than sitting here doing nothing.

RAT: I hoped you'd say that. Come on then. Otter thinks that wherever he is, if he is anywhere, poor little chap, he'll make for the ford. It's where Otter first taught him to swim.

(MOLE *takes the oars, an expert now, and as he rows upstream on this summer evening the moon rises over the meadows and the broad river. Over by the ford a dark figure waits.* RAT *calls to him across the water.*)

(*Calling*) Otter! Otter! Are you there?

OTTER: Yes, I'm here.

RAT: It's Ratty and Mole.

OTTER: Hello. Hello, Moley. Fine night.

MOLE: Any sign?

OTTER: 'Fraid not. Still. Live in hopes. You just taking the air?

RAT: We thought we'd have a scout round. Want to come?

OTTER: I'll stay here if you don't mind. Got a hunch this is where the little chap'll make for.

MOLE: I'm sure he'll turn up.

OTTER: Oh yes. Just a matter of waiting really.

(MOLE *rows on.*)

(*Calling from a distance*) Ratty, Mole. Thank you.

RAT: Funny about children. All the worry. Is it worth it?

MOLE: I know. I wouldn't want any. Me all over again. No fear. Mind you, there were fourteen of us. There was Frank and Claud, Winifred and Jane . . . she got caught in a trap and made into a waistcoat . . . that's one of the risks of being a mole, people are always wanting you for a waistcoat . . . Sorry, where was I?

RAT: Listen, Mole.

MOLE: Sammy and William and Clarence.

60

RAT: Mole. Shut up. Listen.
  (*There is the sound of distant music which at first only* RAT *can hear.*)
MOLE: What is it?
RAT: There . . . can't you hear it? The music.
MOLE: No.
RAT: It's music that I've never heard before and yet I seem to know it.
  (*This of course is the case with lots of music but* RAT, *who has never been to the Wigmore Hall, is not to know that.*)
MOLE: All I can hear is the wind in the willows.
RAT: There it is again. Row, Mole, row. Follow the music. It's meant for us. It's a call. You must hear it now. Moley . . . it's all around.
MOLE: Yes, I do. But it's . . . it's coming from the island above the weir.
RAT: We're going to find him, I'm sure . . .
  (RAT *stands up in the boat for which long ago at their first meeting* MOLE *had been called an idiot.*)
MOLE: Ratty, never stand up in a boat, remember.
RAT: Hang all that. Stop the boat. I must follow the music. It's somewhere. It's here.
  (*They land.*)
MOLE: I feel as if I'm in church. Not that I've ever been in church.
RAT: Hush, Moley. Just hold my hand.
  (*The voice of* PAN *speaks the verse with* RAT *and* MOLE *repeating 'Forget' at the end of each stanza.*)
PAN: Lest the awe should dwell
      And turn your frolic to fret
      You shall look on my power
      At the helping hour
      But then you shall forget.
RAT *and* MOLE: Forget.
PAN: Lest limbs be reddened and rent
      I spring the trap that is set
      As I loose the snare
      You may glimpse me there

For surely you shall forget.

RAT and MOLE: Forget, forget.

PAN: Helper and healer I cheer
       Small waifs in the woodland wet
       Strays I find in it
       Wounds I bind in it
       Bidding them all forget.

RAT and MOLE: Forget.

(*The music fades and the two slightly dazed animals return to reality.*)

MOLE: Look. Here's Portly.

RAT: Fast asleep.

MOLE: There was someone here, Ratty. Some great creature.

RAT: Was there? There was music. I remember the music.

MOLE: Yes. There was music.

RAT: It's gone. Never mind. Come along, Portly. Let's go and find Otter. This sounds like him now.

ALBERT: Oh, does it? Well, you're wrong. Oh, look who it isn't. Mole and Rat.

(MOLE *and* RAT *are still not quite themselves and in the aftermath of such a sacred moment do not quite take in this mundane interruption.*)

'Long time no see, Albert.'

'Where've you been, Albert?'

Well since you ask, I was sold to a gypsy, who beat me.

'Oh dear, Albert, we're sorry to hear that. What did you do?'

I escaped, and now I'm looking for Toad, with whom I have a little bone to pick.

RAT: Toad's locked up.

ALBERT: Oh no he isn't. He ought to be, but he isn't. Toad is out and heading for home. I'm mildly surprised he's not here.

RAT: I hope nothing's happened to him.

MOLE: So do I.

ALBERT: I couldn't bear it.

RAT: But where is he? Where's Toad?

(*They go off as* TOAD *runs on, pursued by all those people and animals he has managed to upset.*)

WEASELS/WILD WOODERS: He talks too loud

He thinks he's clever
We'll put him away for ever and ever.
Where's Toad?
Where's Toad?

RUPERT: He stole our car.

MONICA: It's just not cricket.

TICKET CLERK: He travelled on the railway and didn't buy a
ticket.

ALL: Where's Toad?

TOAD: Oh help.

ALL: Where's Toad?

TOAD: Oh golly.

WASHERWOMAN: He tied me up.
He stole my dress.

BARGEWOMAN: He left my barge in a terrible mess.

ALL: Where's Toad?
Where's Toad?

MAN: He's jolly rich
And that's a plus

ALL HUMANS: But he's not really one of us.

WILD WOODERS: Where's Toad?
Where's Toad?

ALL: He talks too loud
He thinks he's clever
We'll put him away for ever and ever.
Where's Toad?
Where's Toad?
Where's Toad?

A WILD WOODER: There's Toad!

ALL: There's Toad!

(TOAD *is hunted round and round the stage until he finally takes
shelter in Rat's doorway.*)

RAT, *apron on, is preparing supper for* MOLE *and* BADGER, *who are
obviously overdue.*

RAT: Moley! Badger! Is that you? I've been so worried.

(TOAD *bursts in and motions him to silence until the sound of
pursuit fades.*)

TOAD: Given them the slip again! The fools! Ratty, my dear
    fellow, how are you?

RAT: Is it Toad?

TOAD: Of course it's Toad. Who else could elude his pursuers in
    so daredevil a fashion?

RAT: What are you dressed in? Is it . . . is it . . . a frock?

TOAD: Oh, this? Yes. It's rather becoming, don't you think?

RAT: Toad. Oh Toad. What has happened to you?

TOAD: Now don't start. I've been back two minutes and you're
    already pulling a long face. When you hear what I've been
    through I think you'll change your tune.
    (BADGER *enters*.)

RAT: Badger, where on earth have you been? Where's Moley?

BADGER: You know where we've been. On patrol.

RAT: But you're so late.

BADGER: Is that Toad? Welcome home, Toad. Alas, what am I
    saying? Oh, unhappy Toad. This is a poor homecoming.
    (*Shaking his head* BADGER *goes and sits at the table and eats a
    pork pie*.)

TOAD: What on earth's the matter with him? Unhappy Toad?
    Why, I've never felt more cheerful in my life . . .
    (MOLE *now comes in and he at least is genuinely pleased to see*
    TOAD *though it's not long before he too heads for the dinner-
    table*.)

MOLE: Toady. I've been looking forward to this. We knew you
    were coming. How are you?

TOAD: Now this is more like it, Moley . . . how did you know I
    was coming?

MOLE: Albert told us.

TOAD: Albert? Who's Albert?

RAT: Albert the horse. Whom you sold, Toad, sold to a gypsy.

MOLE: That wasn't very nice, Toady.

TOAD: Well, he wanted to widen his horizons . . . I wasn't going
    to stand in his way.

RAT: You sold him for some stew, Toad, and he would have
    ended up in the knacker's yard. Fortunately he escaped.

TOAD: Escaped? That's very irresponsible of him.

MOLE: You must have managed to escape too. You are clever.

RAT: Mole . . .

TOAD: Well, I did, of course, but that was different. But clever? Not really. To break out of the strongest prison in England . . . is that clever? To capture a railway train single-handed and escape on it. Is that clever? Oh no. I'm sure you're all much cleverer than me.

BADGER: Toad.

TOAD: Yes, Badger.

BADGER: Is that a dress?

TOAD: Er . . . yes, Badger.

BADGER: (*Shaking his head*) I thought it was.

RAT: Go up to my bedroom this minute, Toad, and look in my wardrobe. In it you'll find a choice of tweeds. When you've got into something decent bring down that dress and I will burn it.

TOAD: But . . .

BADGER: Toad . . .

TOAD: Yes, Badger.

BADGER: Do as you're told.

(TOAD *goes.*)

And, Toad.

TOAD: Yes, Badger.

BADGER: Have a cold bath while you're about it.

TOAD: (*Whispering to* MOLE) At least you're pleased to see me.

(*A disapproving look from* RAT *sends* TOAD *scuttling off upstairs.*)

BADGER: No improvement there. Have you told him?

RAT: Not yet. Perhaps that'll make him change his tune.

BADGER: I doubt it.

RAT: You were awfully late the pair of you. And you went out without your muffler again, Moley.

BADGER: Oh Rat, don't fuss. Mole's perfectly safe with me. Pork pie, Mole?

MOLE: Yes, please, Badger.

RAT: And chew it.

(TOAD *comes down dressed in* RAT's *tweeds.*)

TOAD: Now. Where shall I start? I imagine the first thing you will all want to know is how I escaped from the deepest dungeon

of the castle, disguised as a glamorous *blanchisseuse*.
(MOLE *and* BADGER *are eating and say nothing.*)

RAT: Toad, don't you see what an awful ass you've been making of yourself? Handcuffed, imprisoned, starved, chased, insulted, and this I find hardest to bear . . . ignominiously flung in the water . . . by a woman.

TOAD: Who told you that?

RAT: Albert.

TOAD: She was a very large woman. However, since none of you seems to be interested in hearing about my adventures or even particularly pleased to see me . . .

MOLE: I am, Toad.

RAT: Don't talk with your mouth full.

TOAD: . . . I propose to stroll gently down to Toad Hall, get rid of these terrible tweeds and resume my old life.

RAT: I don't think there can be any strolling gently down to Toad Hall.

TOAD: Oh, and why not?

RAT: Because if you do 'stroll gently down' then the first thing that will happen will be that a stoat or a weasel will not so gently take a shot at you.

TOAD: Wild Wooders around Toad Hall?

RAT: They're not just around it. They're in it and on it and all over it and have been for months.

TOAD: But this is outrageous! It's my property.

MOLE: They eat your grub and drink your drink and make bad jokes about you.

TOAD: What sort of jokes?

RAT: About prisons and magistrates and policemen. Not funny at all.

MOLE: No, although there was one I heard . . .

TOAD: I don't want to know. You should never have let them get in there in the first place.

RAT: Oh, Toad, you ungrateful beast.

TOAD: I don't care. I come home. Nobody's pleased to see me. Nobody wants to hear about my lovely adventures . . .

MOLE: I do . . .

TOAD: . . . then to cap it all I find the Wild Wooders have taken

66

over my beautiful riverside home. Parts of which date back to the fourteenth century. It's too much. Well, I'm not scared of them even if you are. I'm going down there this minute to sort them out.

BADGER: (*Having finished his dinner*) Toad. Sit down.

TOAD: No, I . . .

BADGER: *Sit down.* You haven't heard the worst of it. Mole and I have just come back from one of our patrols. The weasels must have got word of your return and the guards have been doubled. Toad Hall is now a fortress. It's impregnable.

TOAD: To ordinary folk, yes. But to someone who's stolen a railway train mere child's play.

TOAD:		I'm going down there now.
MOLE:		And I'm coming with you.
RAT:	(*Together*)	No you are not, Mole.
TOAD:		He can if he wants to.
RAT:		Be sensible, Toad.

BADGER: Shut, up the lot of you. There are more ways of capturing a place than by taking it by storm. Now I am going to tell you a great secret. Coming right up in the middle of Toad Hall and leading from the river bank quite near here is an underground passage.

TOAD: Oh, nonsense, Badger. I know every inch of Toad Hall inside and out and there's no such passage. You've been listening to some of the tales they tell in public houses.

BADGER: I wasn't told it in a public house, Toad, for the good reason that I have never been in a public house. It was told me by someone for whom I had an immense respect, your father. He discovered the passage, repaired it and cleaned it out just in case and when he showed it to me he said, 'Don't let my son know about it. He's a good boy . . .

(TOAD *begins to sniffle.*)

. . . only what he's not good at is holding his tongue. But if he's ever in a fix, Badger, you can reveal the secret.'

TOAD: It's not my fault if I am a bit of a talker.

BADGER: I've found out a thing or two lately. There's going to be a big do tonight . . . it's some sort of celebration and all the weasels will be gathered in the dining hall, eating, drinking

and generally carrying on, and, this is the important thing,
with no guns, pistols or anything.

RAT: But that's no good. There'll still be the sentries.

BADGER: Exactly. That's where the secret passage comes in. It
leads right up into the butler's pantry.

TOAD: Of course. That squeaky board. Now I understand.

MOLE: So we then creep out quietly into the butler's pantry . . .

RAT: With our swords and sticks . . .

BADGER: Rush in on them . . .

TOAD: And whack 'em and whack 'em and whack 'em.
(TOAD *rushes round and round the room jumping over the chairs
and felling imaginary adversaries.*)

RAT: When do we move?

BADGER: Tonight. And it will be a hard-fought fight, so I for one
am going to take a nap. I suggest you all do the same.
(BADGER *puts a handkerchief over his face and settles down.*)

RAT: I'm still worried about those sentries.

Which is a cue for the scene to change to two STOATS *on sentry duty
outside Toad Hall.*

SERGEANT FRED: Now Gerald, what are your orders?

STOAT GERALD: Nobody is to pass, Sergeant Fred, but if anybody
does try to get in then I stop at anything to prevent them. Is
that right?

SERGEANT FRED: More or less. Just keep your eyes peeled.

STOAT GERALD: Yes, Sergeant Fred. Right, Sergeant Fred.
(RAT's *orders to burn the washerwoman's dress must have been
ignored because here comes* MOLE *wearing it.*)
Who comes there?

MOLE: Forgive me for saying so but it should be 'Who goes
there?'

STOAT GERALD: Coming or going, you've no business here.

MOLE: Oh yes, I have. I've come to see if you want any washing
done today.

STOAT GERALD: No, we don't. We don't do any washing on duty.

MOLE: Or any other time, I bet.

SERGEANT FRED: What's the trouble, Gerald? Run away, my
good woman, run away.

MOLE: Don't you my good woman me. And as for running away it won't be me that'll be running away in a very short time from now.

STOAT GERALD: What's she mean, Sergeant Fred?

SERGEANT FRED: Take no notice, Gerald. She don't know what she's talking about.

MOLE: Oh, don't I? Well, let me tell you something. My daughter, she washes for Mr Badger, so I do know what I'm talking about, and you'll know too pretty soon. A hundred bloodthirsty badgers are going to attack Toad Hall this very night.

SERGEANT FRED: A hundred?

MOLE: Armed with rifles. That's via the paddock.

SERGEANT FRED: Thanks very much for telling us. If we all concentrate on the paddock, we'll easily repel 'em.

MOLE: Well, you might. And then you might not. Because that's not all.

STOAT GERALD: Not all? Not all? Oh, Sergeant.

MOLE: Six boatloads of rats with pistols and cutlasses will come up the river and effect a landing in the garden.

SERGEANT FRED: But I can't cope with that.

MOLE: Not to mention the picked body of toads known as the Die-Hards or the Death-or-Glory Toads.

STOAT GERALD: And which way are they coming?

MOLE: Through the orchard. T'ra.

STOAT GERALD: Through the orchard, via the paddock, up the river! We shan't know which way to turn. Oh, Sergeant Fred.

SERGEANT FRED: What?

STOAT GERALD: If my mum sends a note is it all right if I don't come in tonight?

Back in RAT'S *home* BADGER *is still in the armchair reading a newspaper while* RAT, *clipboard in hand, is making separate piles of weapons and equipment.*

RAT: There's a pistol for Badger; there's a pistol for Rat. There's a pistol for Toad; there's a pistol for Mole. There's a lantern for Badger (*etc.*).

BADGER: I'm not criticizing, Rat but once we're past the ferrets on sentry duty, we shan't want any swords or pistols. Surprise is our best weapon. Give me one stick and I can clear the place single-handed.

TOAD: So could I.

RAT: That's all very well, but I prefer to be on the safe side.

BADGER: Anyway time's getting on. You'd better start climbing into all this hardware.

TOAD: Easy peasy!

(*He picks up a stick and starts hitting his imaginary opponents.*)
I'll learn 'em to steal my house. I'll learn 'em. I'll learn 'em.

RAT: Toady. That's not your pile. This is your pile. And don't say 'Learn 'em'. It's not good English.

BADGER: What are you always nagging at Toad for? What's the matter with his English? It's the same as what I use myself and if it's good enough for me, it ought to be good enough for you.

RAT: All I'm saying, Badger, is that I think it ought to be teach 'em, not learn 'em.

BADGER: But we don't want to teach 'em, do we? The time for teaching 'em's past. We want to learn 'em.

RAT: Oh, very well. You know best. Can't seem to do anything right these days.

(RAT *goes back to his weapon division only now he's saying* (*and rather gloomily*) –)
Teach 'em. Learn 'em. Learn 'em. Teach 'em.

(MOLE *comes in.*)
Moley, where've you been? And *you've* got that frock on now. What is happening?

MOLE: I've been to Toad Hall, putting the wind up the sentries. I told them the place was going to be attacked by hundreds of bloodthirsty badgers and hordes of stop-at-nothing toads.

TOAD: Oh, you silly ass, Mole. You've gone and spoilt everything.

RAT: For once, Moley, I think Toad's right.

(MOLE *is crestfallen and looks at* BADGER *for his verdict.*)

BADGER: Can I ask what effect this news had on the sentries?

MOLE: They were very upset and started running this way and

70

that and saying they wouldn't know which way to turn. I'm
sorry, Badger. I thought I was doing the right thing.

BADGER: Mole, you were doing the right thing. They'll have been
completely demoralized. First sign of trouble and they'll be
off back to the Wild Wood. You have more sense in your
little finger than some other animals have in the whole of
their fat bodies.

TOAD: There's no need to get personal.

(*A cuckoo-clock chimes.*)

BADGER: Zero hour.

RAT: Moley, old chap. Whatever Badger says, I think it's going to
be a pretty big show this evening and I just want you to know
that if anything happens to me I wouldn't have missed it for
the world. Good luck, old chap. Do well.

(*The two friends shake hands, differences settled. Were there time
for a snatch of 'The Dam Busters' it would not be inappropriate.
TOAD now emerges in a makeshift suit of armour that includes a
colander as helmet, a tureen cover as breastplate and as a
codpiece a large jam-strainer.*)

MOLE: Ready, Toad?

TOAD: I certainly am.

RAT: One last thing. Sticking plaster for Mole. Sticking plaster
for Toad. Sticking plaster for . . .

(BADGER *enters and far from being in battle array is still in his
old dressing-gown without even a pistol.*)

Badger, where's all your kit?

BADGER: I've told you, I don't need any. I'm going to do all that
has to be done with this here stick.

RAT: But take some sticking plaster. Just for my sake.

BADGER: Oh, very well. But remember (*He takes a lantern*) our
biggest weapon is surprise. Now I shall go first, then Mole,
Rat next and Toad last.

TOAD: Last? I think I ought to go first. After all it's my house.

BADGER: Toad. Behave. And if you chatter or do anything silly I
shall be seriously angry and you'll be sent back. Surprise,
remember.

TOAD: Surprise, yes. Surprise, you fellows. Surprise.

BADGER: Sssh.

(BADGER *shushes* MOLE *and* MOLE *shushes* RAT *and* RAT
shushes TOAD *and* TOAD *shushes the room in general. They set off
down the passage but* TOAD *is impeded by his armour.*)

RAT: All right ahead? Come on, Toad. Keep up.
(*Hurrying to catch up* TOAD *careers into* RAT *who falls over*
MOLE *who bumps into* BADGER.)

BADGER: What's this? Attacked from the rear. Down Mole, down
Rat. Hold or I fire.

TOAD: No. no. Don't shoot. Don't shoot. It's only me.

BADGER: Toad. We are on active service. You are under orders
and you have disobeyed them. You have jeopardized the
whole expedition. I am going to send you back.
(TOAD *starts wailing.*)

TOAD: Don't want to be sent back. It's not fair. It's my house. It's
my passage. I won't go back. I won't.

MOLE: Give him another chance, Badger. He'll be all right once
we get into the fight.

RAT: Without him there'll only be three of us.

BADGER: Very well, but, Toad, it's the last time, do you
understand?

TOAD: Yes, Badger.

BADGER: These people mean business.
(*They go further and as they get nearer the Hall begin to hear the
noise of the party and the sound of the weasels.*)

TOAD: Oh dear, I've suddenly remembered. I came out without
my handkerchief, I'll just . . .

BADGER: Toad.
(*Any number of weasels is preferable to the wrath of* BADGER *so*
TOAD *presses on until they reach the trapdoor under the butler's
pantry, heave it up and find themselves standing in the pantry
next door to the weaselly function.*)

*The dining room at Toad Hall is furnished with a long table along
which the* WILD WOODERS *are sprawled in varying stages of
intoxication and utter decadence. On the wall hangs a huge tapestry
portraying one of* TOAD's *ancestors, depicted as a naked cherub in a
woodland setting. Beginning in a low monotone then rising to a furious
crescendo the* WILD WOODERS *chant their hatred of Toad.*

ALL: He talks too loud
    He thinks he's clever.
    We'll put him away for ever and ever
    Where's Toad?

    He talks too loud
    He thinks he's clever
    We'll put him away for ever and ever
    Where's Toad?

    There's Toad!
    (*They all point at the tapestry and throw themselves about in
    dissipated merriment.* WEASEL NORMAN *now rises.*)
WEASEL NORMAN: I now call upon our beloved chairman to give
    his report.
CHAIRMAN WEASEL: When Stoat, Weasel, Ferret, Fox and
    Company moved into Toad Hall it was a typical English
    country estate, run on traditional lines . . . comfortable,
    hospitable . . . and making no profit at all. Three months of
    what you might call calculated decrepitude have
    considerably reduced its market value and since the owner is
    now a convicted felon your directors are convinced they can
    legally acquire the property at a knockdown price.
    (BADGER, RAT, MOLE *and* TOAD *have stolen in from behind the
    tapestry.*)
TOAD: Oh are they! Well, I'll show them.
BADGER: Steady, Toad. Not yet.
CHAIRMAN WEASEL: Our plan now is to convert Toad Hall into a
    nice mix of executive apartments and office accommodation,
    shove on a marina, and a café or two to fetch in the
    tourists . . .
BADGER: Oh, the horror! The horror!
CHAIRMAN WEASEL: . . . and once we've done that we're
    confident that this run-down stately home can be made a
    viable commercial enterprise as the Toad Hall Park and
    Leisure Centre.
    (*Whether this is a good tactical moment or not* BADGER *can stand
    these terrible revelations no longer and orders his little band to
    attack.*)

73

BADGER: At 'em, lads. At 'em.

(*The* WILD WOODERS *put up a good fight but are no match for our heroes. Many flee and the few remaining are rounded up.*)

BADGER: Now, my excellent and deserving Mole, I want you to form these rather sorry-looking fellows into a fatigue party and make them give this place a thorough going over.

MOLE: Come on, you heard the gentleman. Jump to it.

RAT: That's right. And see they sweep under the beds, put clean sheets and pillowcases on, and remembering particularly to turn down one corner of the bedclothes in the time-honoured manner. I want a can of hot water, clean towels and fresh cakes of soap in every room and a tin of biscuits by each bed.

BADGER: Excellent, Ratty. I'm reluctant to say it but this victory of ours seems to me to call for some kind of celebration.

RAT: I quite agree.

MOLE: Rather!

TOAD: You mean a party? I'm very good at parties.

RAT: Good. Then you can write the invitations and send them off straightaway.

TOAD: I don't want to stop indoors writing mouldy old invitations . . . I want to go round my property and tell everyone the news.

BADGER: Toad.

TOAD: I eat every word. Write the invitations I shall this minute. I know just how the proceedings should go. What I think would be appropriate would be a few remarks about our prison system, followed by some thoughts on the state of our railways which would lead naturally into a short disquisition on England's inland waterways . . . possibly ending with a song . . . no?

(BADGER, RAT *and* MOLE *are silent.*)

Too serious?

(*Silence.*)

Too . . . funny?

BADGER: There must be no speeches.

TOAD: Just what I was thinking. People don't want to be lectured. I'll stick to my songs.

(*Silence.*)

No songs?

RAT: No. And we are not arguing with you, Toad. We are telling
you.

TOAD: (*Resignedly*) No songs.

MOLE: Mayn't he sing just one little song?

RAT: No. It's for your own good, Toady. You know you're going
to have to turn over a new leaf sooner or later and this will be
a splendid time to do it. It will be a turning point in your
career.

(TOAD *thinks hard*.)

TOAD: My friends. It was just a small thing that I asked . . .
merely leave to blossom and expand for the last time, just
once more to hear that tumultuous applause that always
seems to me somehow to bring out my best qualities, but you
are right, I know, and I am wrong. My friends, henceforth I
will be a very different toad. I solemnly promise. You shall
never have occasion to blush for me again. But oh dear, oh
dear . . . this is a hard world.

MOLE: Poor Toady.

RAT: I know. I feel a brute.

BADGER: It's the only way.

RAT: If he is going to live here and be respected he must learn to
fit in. If you can do it, Mole, so can he.

(*They leave* TOAD *to himself but* MOLE *turns back with a word
of comfort.*)

MOLE: I'm sorry, Toady. I shall miss your songs.

(TOAD, *left alone, takes off his armour and rights a few of the
chairs overturned in the battle. With the empty chairs as his
audience and in a sad and broken voice he gives his last
recitation.*)

TOAD: A Recitation
By Toad
Entitled,
The Toad Came Home.

There was panic in the parlour and howling in the hall,
There was crying in the cowshed and shrieking in the stall
When the Toad came home

When the Toad came home
There was smashing in of window and crashing in of door
There was chivvying in of weasels and fainting on the floor
When the Toad came home.

Bang go the drums
The trumpeters are tooting and the soldiers are saluting
And the cannon they are shooting and the motor cars are
   hooting
As the Hero . . . comes.

Shout Hooray
And let each one of the crowd try and shout it very loud
In honour of an animal of whom you're justly proud
For it's Toad's great day.
(*He modestly acknowledges the non-existent tributes from the*
non-existent audience.)
Thank you, thank you. Most kind, most kind.
And so at this turning point in his fortunes Toad
acknowledges the applause but with that modesty he will
never henceforth abandon he begins his new life.

TOAD's *party takes the form of a garden fête in the grounds of Toad*
Hall and the stage fills with all the creatures of the River Bank. The
rabbits are there, the hedgehogs and even the weasels, who have been
put in pinnies and hats for the occasion and as 'tweenies' go round
shamefacedly with trays of snacks.
   There is music and TOAD, *very much the host, moves among the*
crowds with greetings for everyone.
TOAD: Ratty, may I present the gaoler's daughter, who single-
   handed effected my escape from prison.
GAOLER'S DAUGHTER: Oh Toady, you little love. (*She kisses him.*
   TOADY *is not at all abashed by this kiss, and why should he be?*
   Someone who has had crazes for houseboats and caravans and
   motors is quite likely to have a craze for girls. And just as TOAD
   wanted to initiate RAT *into the charms of caravanning so he*
   wants to introduce him to the delight of kissing.)
TOAD: Ratty kicked the weasels out of Toad Hall. I think he
   deserves a kiss too.

RAT: No, no. Please.
>   (RAT *is most reluctant and is covered in embarrassment but the*
>   GAOLER'S DAUGHTER *kisses him nevertheless and with*
>   *unexpected consequences.*)
>   Oh. I say. That's not unpleasant. I think my friend Mole
>   might like that. Moley. Try this.
>   (*So* MOLE *gets a kiss too and perhaps his kiss is longer and more*
>   *lingering.*)
>   What do you think?

MOLE: Mmmm. Yes.

RAT: Yes. I think one could get quite used to that.
>   (*Life, one may imagine, is never going to be quite the same again*
>   *– at least for* RAT *and* MOLE.)

MOLE: What about Badger?

RAT: I don't think it's Badger's thing at all.

TOAD: Badger, you must meet the gentleman who drove the train
>   which I escaped on.

BADGER: I thought you drove the train.

TOAD: Me? Whatever gave you that idea? No, no. And here's Alfred!

ALBERT: (*Who is giving one of the baby rabbits a ride*) Albert.

TOAD: I owe you an apology.

ALBERT: No, don't apologize or I shall have nothing to be
>   depressed about.

TOAD: And you too, my dear Bargeperson. All of you contributed
>   to my escape and without you I would not be standing here
>   today.
>   (*The cheerful hubbub is suddenly stilled by the appearance of a*
>   POLICEMAN, *followed by the* MAGISTRATE.)

PC: Are you Mr Toad of Toad Hall in the County of Berkshire?

TOAD: I am.

PC: Convicted of taking and driving away a motor car and
>   sentenced to twenty years' imprisonment?

TOAD: (*Stricken*) Yes. Yes. That's me.

MAGISTRATE: And do you still do kedgeree for breakfast with
>   devilled kidneys on the side?

TOAD: I do.

MAGISTRATE: Then I order you to be pardoned without a stain on
>   your tablecloth!

(*There is general rejoicing together with shouts of 'Speech, Speech'*.)

TOAD: No, no speech. I'm just so happy to see you enjoying Toad Hall and its gardens. I'd like in the future to share it with you not only as a house but as a venue for all sorts of occasions . . . Opera perhaps . . .

LISTENERS: Opera?

TOAD: Chamber concerts . . .

(*These ideas go down less than well with the crowd, who begin to quieten down.*)

Even, if we're lucky, actors with one-man shows.

BADGER: (*Disgustedly*) Actors!

TOAD: Who knows, Toad Hall might one day have its very own arts festival.

(*Disappointed by this new* TOAD *the crowd starts to drift away.*)

RABBIT ROSE: Tell us about the fight. Give us a song.

OTHERS: Yes! Give us a song, Toady! Tell us about the fight!

TOAD: No, no. I have nothing to say about that. Badger was the mastermind, Mole and Rat did the fighting and I merely served in the ranks and did what I was told.

(*The celebrations go on as* BADGER, RAT *and* MOLE *stroll downstage.*)

MOLE: Toad is better now, isn't he?

RAT: Oh yes. Completely cured.

BADGER: I wouldn't have believed it if I'd not seen it. But it's true. Look at him. He's an altered toad.

MOLE: And he is better? I mean . . . *improved*.

RAT: Well of course he's better. He's learned to behave himself. No more crazes. No more showing off. He's one of us.

MOLE: Yes.

BADGER: What is it, little Mole?

MOLE: I just thought . . . I just thought that now he's more like everybody else, it's got a bit dull.

RAT: I'd try not to think like that if I were you, Moley.

MOLE: No?

RAT: It doesn't do.

(BADGER *nods his head in agreement as* TOAD *joins them.*)

TOAD: I say, Ratty, why didn't you tell me before?

RAT: Tell you what?

TOAD: About not showing off, being humble and shy and nice.

RAT: I did tell you.

TOAD: Yes, but what you didn't say was that this way I get more attention than ever. Everybody loves me! It's wonderful!

RAT, MOLE and BADGER: Oh, Toad!

(*The cast now join in a Circassian Circle dance and having taken their bows (*TOAD *feigning great reluctance) they form up again and with the weasels as a backing group (singing 'Wack dabbety do') there is a final reprise of 'Ducks' Ditty'.*)

Chapter 5

1   A. Patrick Purnell, S.J., *Our Faith Story*, Collins, London, 1985, p.28.
2   Tony Bridge, *Road to Damascus*, Thames TV Broadcast, 1986.

Chapter 7

1   *All are Called*, Church House, Publishing, London, 1986. p.8.
2   Wolfgang Bartholomäus, *Being a Christian in the Church and the World of Tomorrow* Concilium 174 *The Transmission of the Faith to the Next Generation*, T. (T. Clark Ltd., Edinburgh, 1984. p.83.

Notes

Chapter 1

1   *Rite of Christian Initiation of Adults*, Geoffrey Chapman, a division of Cassell Publishers Ltd., London, 1987, p.5. Copyright ICEL.

Chapter 2

1   John Shea, *Stories of Faith*, Thomas Moore Press, Chicago, 1980, p.43.

Chapter 3

1   Norbert Mette, *The Christian Community's Task in the Process of Religious Education*. Concilium 174. *The Transmission of the Faith to the Next Generation*. T. & T. Clark Ltd. Edinburgh, 1984. p.73.
2   John Westerhoff III, *A Pilgrim People*, Seabury Press, Minneapolis, 1984, p.1.
3   Karen Hinman Powell, *Beginnings Institute* Conference Papers, North American Forum on the Catechumenate, 1986.

Chapter 4

1   John Westerhoff III, *Building God's People*, Seabury Press, New York, 1983, p.117.